Happy B

Augush

CATHRYN PETIT

Sisters of the Silk Veil: A Troupe Emerges

Dear Sally,

I hope you enjoy this first novel in the series, Sisters of the Silk Veil!

Cathryn Petit

First published by Cathryn's Cadence 2019

Copyright © 2019 by Cathryn Petit

This novel is entirely a work of fiction. The names, characters and incidents portrayed in it are the work of the author's imagination. Any resemblance to actual persons, living or dead, events or localities is entirely coincidental.

The fictional town of Southbridge, FL described in this novel was inspired by St. Augustine, FL.

First edition

ISBN: 978-1-7331382-0-8

Editing by Susan Edwards
Cover art by Lesley Worrell

This book was professionally typeset on Reedsy.
Find out more at reedsy.com

To the memory of my beloved husband, Bob, with whom I spent three joyful months in St. Augustine, FL.

Contents

One

A Shopping Trip Does Not a Saturday Make

"*A* picture of one of the houses you're going to die in was up on your computer screen," Josh said as he entered the kitchen with his laptop . "I shut it down for you."

"Oh, thanks," Jewell said, as she watched the Fox Sparrows and Horned Larks, two of the species capable of enduring the northwest winters. They fluttered about the branches snatching seeds from the feeder as though life were some simple and joyous proposition. Months earlier, she had fastened the feeder to a high limb by hanging out the window of their upstairs apartment. The valiant effort made more for Josh's enjoyment than hers.

"Do you ever think about trying another doctor?" she asked, studying the birds.

No answer.

"Coffee?" She stood to retrieve another cup for herself.

"Sure, if you're buying."

She feigned amusement with a slight smile as she bent to pet Romeo who had followed her to the coffee pot. She knew Josh

1

heard the question.

"How's my big boy?" She sank her fingers deep into the standard poodle's black curls. His puffy top piled high, per her instructions to the groomer.

Jewell poured, sweetened and lightened the coffees, hers sweeter and lighter than his. She drew comfort from the Victorian kitchen. It was her favorite room with its antique baker's cabinet, the cast-iron sink, and those windows nearly floor to ceiling.

After delivering Josh's coffee, she went back to the counter, leaned against it and cupped her mug to savor the essence.

Another Saturday like the rest lay ahead. The shopping trip was shaping up to be the highlight of her week. She would imagine and envy the lives of the other shoppers, who were, no doubt, living fuller lives with their adventures and friends.

Had it always been like this? She racked her brain to remember other Saturdays. Saturdays before...well, before he had gotten so bad.

"Want me to make you some breakfast?" Josh asked. "You know, chocolate cereal does not a breakfast make."

"No thanks. I'll grab something later."

"Well at least sit at the table again."

Jewell returned to the rustic chunky table with its high-back chairs and resumed gazing out the window as Josh typed.

"Are you going to answer my question?"

"No. No more doctors," he said.

"Can't we talk about it?"

"Are you bound and determined to ruin our weekend?"

"Don't you want to get better?"

"Of course I do. If I could go outside without freaking out, I'd love it. But, it would be the same as all the other times. I take the medicine, it works for a little while until my brain gets so foggy I can't function, I can't write. And don't even get me started on the counseling. Worthless."

"Maybe we could find something better. You can't even get past the front door now."

"For hell's sake, Jewell, I don't want to talk about it. I'm happy the way things are."

"Well aren't you the lucky one? I'm just so happy for you. How peachy. But what about me?" She hit her chest, her cheeks ablaze.

"What about you?"

Romeo barked at their raised voices.

"Do I look happy?" she asked. "Do you think this 800-square-foot-prison makes me happy? I go out to work five days a week and to the grocery store on Saturday. Whoopee. I'm only twenty-seven years old."

She didn't wait for a reply. She grabbed the cloth grocery bags, slipped into her rain boots and took off.

∞∞∞

Yep, Jewell thought, looking at the drab Washington sky as she headed for her car. Not much different from the day before or even the week before. She predicted the lineup of clouds promised sunshine about as much as the, The Cookie Diet, promised weight loss. She was, if nothing else, a practical scientist and skeptical of weight loss from fad diets and sunshine from drab skies. Still, she held out hope for at least a sliver of sun.

The correlation between the dreary weather and her dreary life didn't escape her. She recognized her dullness in sweat pants, gray rain boots, and pulled-back hair. Fussing over her pretty blonde ringlets never entered the equation. What was the point? Gussy up for an entire weekend sequestered in their apartment?

Sequestered, yes, that was the word.

She exited her silk-blue Volkswagen Beetle, a color she had selected when Josh gave her some of the settlement money and encouraged her to order a new car. Even though he wasn't raised by his mother, he was her only next of kin and therefore became the beneficiary of a wrongful death lawsuit when she, along with all the other patients in the dialysis center that day, died after receiving the wrong fluids.

Choosing the car and the color had constituted the highlight of the past year. She had reeled with excitement when the car was ready for pickup, only to have her joy dashed when Josh bailed on her. She had gone alone.

The salesman had instructed her to pose in front of the car as he snapped a picture with her phone. He had instructed her to smile, but she didn't. The photo was later deleted.

Jewell snatched a grocery cart and made her way through the familiar aisles. Couples shopping together struck her the most. She viewed the tall slender man in pressed pants and polo shirt with his equally tall and slender partner. She, unlike Jewell, had styled her hair for the outing. Whether wife or girlfriend mattered little what mattered was their unity, the sheer beauty of doing simple everyday tasks together.

She touched his shoulder as they perused the many selections of wine. He pulled a bottle from the shelf for her inspection. The woman with the styled hair gave her seal of approval with a nod and smile. He added six bottles to the cart.

Yep, a dinner party made further evident by the packs of shrimp, those fancy crackers Jewell always wanted to try, and the fresh-cut flowers. She imagined these parties where friends gathered, glasses of fine wine in hand as they discussed the books they had read and plays they had attended. They all enjoyed more

4

interesting lives, or so it seemed to a girl on the outside looking in.

As Jewell ambled down the aisle containing the boxes of gooey, sugary, individually wrapped cakes, she placed her forearm on the shelf, knocking boxes into her cart. She was going to need a slew of sweets to withstand the weekend. Thank heavens for at least one useful thing she had inherited from her parents, a speedy metabolism. Oh yeah, and her genius IQ: 160 was the number assigned.

In a rote manner, she plodded trance-like through the shopping motions until she spotted Taylor, a coworker from the lab. Well, not a true coworker since Jewell was a scientist and Taylor an administrative assistant to the director of research. In any event, they both worked for Oliver and Timpelton Labs.

Jewell abandoned her weekly shopping drill at the sight of Taylor.

Her eyes darted back and forth. Where could she hide? Could she drop behind the cart? This plan would work until Taylor passed her cart and spied her crouched on the floor. What would she say? Oh, I was tying my shoelaces? No, she had on boots for heavens sakes. "These stupid boots," she murmured, regretting the decision to carelessly throw them on as she left the apartment.

At the other end, Taylor stood analyzing the life out of some label, probably some health food crap. But Taylor's probing of the contents in hand bought time to devise a plan. The end aisle, she thought.

The natural progression of most shoppers was to progress through the store to the left. So she calculated Taylor would progress similarly, plus she had come from the right.

Taylor moved. Jewell dashed behind the end aisle and flattened her back against it as if thrust into some covert mission. She intermittently peeked down the aisle to track Taylor's where-abouts. Her heart pounded. The last thing she needed was the cute put-together Taylor getting a gander of her in this state of frumpiness.

A gentleman Jewell guessed to be in his seventies approached her. "You okay, honey?"

She waved him on dismissively and periodically peeked down the aisle to track Taylor.

He didn't leave. "I said, you need something?"

Jewell remained silent and attempted to nudge him on with a toss of her head and a roll of her eyes in the same direction for extra measure.

A woman close to the man's age rounded the corner pushing a cart. She addressed the man loudly, similar to the way someone hard of hearing would. They appeared to be a couple. "WHAT'S WRONG WITH HER?" the woman shouted to the man.

"WHAT'S WRONG WITH YOU? DO YOU NEED HELP?" she shouted at Jewell, not waiting for the man's response.

Jewell sneaked another peek down the aisle and found Taylor gone. She threw her arms in the air and shook her head in exasperation at the concerned couple, and then made her way to an earlier aisle. She cowered in place to allow Taylor time to progress through the store. She hoped Taylor wouldn't find it necessary to loop back around for any forgotten items.

She didn't.

Taylor epitomized the office beauty queen; every office had one, and the prospect of an encounter with her intimidated Jewell. If only she had devoted time to her makeup, clothes, and hair, the degree of intimidation would be less. Taylor, who flitted about the office in her designer tight skirts and alluring heels, with her perfect hair and makeup, wouldn't shy away from any encounters.

Jewell determined enough time had lapsed for Taylor to forge well ahead and deemed it safe to resume shopping.

At the checkout line, Jewell fumbled through magazines to pass the time. It was a long line. She grabbed the magazine with the most intriguing cover. It read: "Top Ten Party Ideas." The cover photo showed groups of people in brightly colored clothing on a well-manicured lawn. They appeared to be involved in easy conversations and laughter. It showed a close-up of the pleased hostess in the forefront, arms folded and giving a wink.

Jewell sensed the presence of someone close behind her. She turned with a startle.

Taylor stood behind her, peering over her shoulder. "Nice party. You know, I bet if a person wanted to make friends and be invited to a party like that one they'd have to quit avoiding people."

Taylor wheeled around in her light-blue shoes, pumps the color of robin eggs, causing her blonde bobbed hair to swish as she marched away.

Humph, Jewell thought, what does she know? She has all the friends she could ever want.

∞∞∞

The trip home was a short one. She contemplated driving awhile to avoid going straight home, but like every time before, she went home. The apartment door flung open and Romeo leapt at her as if she had been gone for days.

"I know, buddy, you need to go out."

"Sorry," Josh called from the kitchen.

"No problem. I'll walk him after I bring the groceries in."

"Sorry I can't help there either."

"No worries."

The weekend played out as usual. Josh made a decadent dinner with the ingredients Jewell brought home. She thought of the Groundhog Day movie and how their days seemed to play out the same, over and over. She sat at the antique kitchen table and watched Josh cook as she petted Romeo.

"You're such a cute poodle-head," she said in her best baby talk, something that never failed to set Romeo's tail wagging.

"Did you get much writing done this week?" she asked Josh.

"Enough. I met the deadlines for my articles. Not much on the novel, though. Did you check your investments? Mine went down."

"What do you think?"

"Of course you did."

"Of course I did. I moved my funds when I noted the downward trend. I told you, I can monitor yours if you want."

Jewell left the kitchen chair to sit on the floor with Romeo. He laid as much of his sixty-pound body over her as possible. He seemed to believe he was still the puppy she had rescued three years earlier.

The succulent fragrance of sauteing garlic filled the room.

"Josh, I'm sorry about this morning."

"Me too."

She hung her head. Josh's reluctance for treatment reinforced the solidity of her entrapment. There would be no escape. No adventure to another town where she could start over. She believed if only she could escape Port Eastlyn, Washington, where she grew up and had such a rough time, happiness would follow.

The usual course of the weekend continued into the evening as they watched their favorite classic movies.

Later, Jewell retired to the bedroom computer where she explored towns online, places where she imagined capturing her freedom. She preferred to search the Internet away from Josh. He was aware she fantasized about living elsewhere, but he didn't realize to what degree her searching had progressed.

They had an ongoing joke. Josh said he refused to leave the apartment and how he would die there. She said she refused to die in the apartment and searched vigorously for another home to die in. If only she had known how true part of the joke rang.

Two

A Tale of Two Friends; A Tale of Two Lovers

With another weekend behind her, Jewell meandered to work Monday morning.

From an early age, she had loved to submerge herself into her studies, especially science. She found further escape in experiments. Being a scientific genius made it a breeze to graduate with honors in the master's program. This aided her in landing a research job and later project manager position at the local pharmaceutical company.

Much like all aspects of Jewell's life, both past, and present, she had few friends at work. There were the proverbial "cool ones" and then there were Jewell and Erin.

Erin was one of the production technicians. She was a cynical girl who had her own issues with fitting in. However, unlike Jewell, Erin displayed no discernible desire to fit in and make friends. Jewell figured Erin took some comfort in Jewell being in the same boat.

"How was your weekend?" Erin asked.

"The same as usual," Jewell said.

"Mine too."

"I ran into Taylor at the grocery store."

"Egad, you didn't talk to Miss Priss, did you?"

"Well, she interjected herself into my space and commented on the magazine I was looking at, implying something about making friends."

"Don't pay any attention to her." Erin said and changed the subject, "Um, how's Josh?"

"Worse."

Erin was the only one Jewell had confided in regarding Josh's agoraphobia.

"Why don't you dump him? You two aren't married with kids or anything. How long have you been together?"

"You mean dump him like a pair of worn socks; you mean leave him before I make sure he is competent to live alone?"

"No. I guess not."

"And we've been together twelve years."

She thought of her entangled life with Josh. They had been glued together since the first day Jewell entered the new high school in her freshman year.

She had walked into the room and sized up the crowd, deciding where to take her place. It was the kind of setup forcing a girl with wide-rimmed glasses and blemished skin to steer away from the back rows where the cheerleader sat with her long glistening hair so silky the cascade flowed like a waterfall. Or the dark curly-haired one in the tight sweater displaying her long legs, as she commanded attention from the gaggle of boys around her.

Ha! Jewell had scoffed to herself as she basked in her superior comprehension of biology. How stereotypically primal they're behaving. They think themselves suave when it boils down to the basic drive for the procreation of the species, the young male eager to plant his seed in fertile soil. They're being led by instinct and not higher cognition. Jewell had more important ambitions.

No, the front of the room was the place for her, where she spotted the equally nerdy redheaded boy, a little pudgy in his outdated striped vest. They must position themselves ahead of the others. The front row allowed closer interaction with the instructor who could impart wisdom. Who needed the social drivel from the back rows?

He had smiled a knowing smile as she approached the desk next to him. "I'm Josh, Josh Anderson."

She unloaded her books on the empty desk. "I'm Jewell, Jewell Caldwell."

From their first greetings on, Jewell and Josh had spent the majority of their hours together in books and movies. How they loved to meet on Saturdays at the matinee to watch and critique old classics while their counterparts watched vampire and zombie movies. The pair viewed their favorites so many times they recited the dialogue along with the characters.

Jewell's love for old classics had led to her first job at the town theater her sophomore year of high school. It was a theater as classic as the movies it showed.

This was the year she had ditched her wide-rimmed glasses and blemished skin with the help of contacts and a miracle skin concoction. Not to mention how a little extra money had prompted a new interest in clothing.

Her mind drifted to one particular spring evening when her relationship with Josh had taken a memorable turn. She wore a dress inspired by the warming air, a dress she stumbled upon at the town consignment shop. She recalled her submergence into femininity as the floral dress blew playfully about her thighs in the spring breeze. For the first time, men stopped to admire her, an unfamiliar happening and it caused her to blush.

Josh frequently walked with Jewell to her home, yet on this day, the trip turned monumental. He stood in the theater lobby stunned still and silent by her metamorphosis. The way he reached to hold her hand was uncharacteristic. She remembered how her hand warmed and tingled as blood pooled. Wetness gathered between their palms. The pair who could converse for hours on end couldn't drum up one word between them.

They had walked in the new silence, eyes straight ahead until they reached the porch of the home later crowned her final foster home.

She called back every moment like it was yesterday and luxuriated in the memory. How he had placed his arms around the arch of her back and pulled her into his warm body gently. She watched him close his eyes.

Sure, Jewell's body had experienced the same stirrings as any other teenage girl. She fantasized about her first kiss, but of all the times she had dreamed of this colossal kiss, Josh held no stake in her fantasies other than how she would run to him to spill the details the following day.

Regardless of previous thoughts, she then stood face to face with her best friend, their bodies pressed so tight, light particles couldn't pass between them. Her stirrings were alive and pulsating.

She had rested her arms over his shoulders. It prompted him to pull her tighter. She braced herself against the spinning porch as the blood left her head and surged into her lower body. He leaned his lips closer to hers and awaited her response. Her mouth watered. She offered no hesitation as she pressed her lips against his soft full lips.

"Jewell," Erin called and snapped her back to the present. "You're a million miles away. I asked about lunch today. Want to go out or order in?"

"Huh? Oh, it doesn't matter to me."

"Okay, let's order in and we can talk about the others in the cafeteria."

"Fine. I need to concentrate on work now. We're making strides with the new drug."

∞∞∞

"How long do they think this thing will last?" Erin unwrapped her deli sandwich and referred to the couple engaged in the new company romance.

Jewell looked up from her cell phone, "What?"

"Jim and Sarah. How long do they really think the relationship will last? I mean, he left his wife for her."

"Oh, who knows? They deserve each other."

"And what about Casey's hair? Hello, time for a root job. Wait, are you even listening? Are you texting with Josh?"

Jewell had lost interest in the catty lunches she and Erin originally embarked upon. When Jewell began working at the lab, Erin approached her early on and struck up a friendship, albeit an unhealthy friendship. At the time, Jewell had no desire to branch out and make additional friends, but things changed.

Perhaps the change inside of Jewell was brought about by the numerous isolated weekends. Whatever the reason, she now longed for connections with others. She longed for friendships with people her age who went out and had fun.

"Yes, I'm texting with Josh. I'm his only link to the outside world."

"Well, you are my only link *within* the outside world." Erin picked up her sandwich, dropped it in the trash and left the cafeteria.

Three

A Cursory Agreement

fter work, Jewell pulled into the driveway of the expansive pink Victorian home. It sat off the road, hidden by towering trees surrounding three sides. She observed the innocent house and wondered how anything so aesthetically pleasing could inflict such misery. Yet there it sat, the vessel separating her from happiness.

It was a house vast enough to hold three families. The first-floor apartment spanned the entire bottom half of the home. The upstairs held two apartments. Jewell and Josh occupied one of the upstairs apartments and the other had sat vacant for some time.

Frank and Karyn, the older couple from the first-floor apartment, were camping enthusiasts. The thirty-foot RV parked in the yard constituted the measuring tool for whether they were home or abroad.

The apartment had an abundance of charm inside with ginger-bread trim and high ceilings. Although Jewell was never quite sure it encompassed enough charm to make up for the drafts and creaky floorboards, Josh had always loved the apartment.

They dined in silence for the most part. What was there to talk about, each day identical to the other, his in the apartment writing and hers in the lab?

Still, Josh looked up often during dinner. He continued to look at her adoringly after all these years. He praised her soft, fair features, her hazel eyes, and her slender body.

Jewell took a gulp of water as she prepared to break the silence. "Josh, I've been thinking."

"Oh no."

"No, I'm serious. I don't want to spark another argument, but as I told you before, the project I chose to work on is an anti-depressant also designed to treat phobias. The drug is in the final year, final months actually, of phase three. It will certainly reach FDA approval soon. The participants in the study are getting incredible results."

"So what?" His tone stiffened.

"The data shows promise. That's so what. Honestly, your resistance to seek help is exasperating."

"I'm sorry. I'm not going to another doctor and go through the whole ordeal again, or the counseling. I thought we hashed this out this past weekend. Plus you said I didn't qualify for the study because of my family history of renal failure."

"No, you didn't qualify and besides, recruitment and enrollment have been closed for some time. You ought to have the hang of my studies by now." She shot him a glance and minutely shook her head.

"I'm not trying to recommend you go to a doctor either. The participants in the experimental arm, the ones actually taking the medication, are meeting the goals of the study with very few side effects. I could bring some home and monitor you. Don't you want to go out into the world?"

"Sure, I repeat, if I could go outside without freaking out."

"Let's at least try it."

"No. And I don't want to talk about it."

He sighed and his face softened. He reached across the table for Jewell's hand. "I'm sure you realize how I worship you. Hell, I hit the lottery the day you sat next to me in the ninth grade. I would and will do anything for you, but not this."

∞∞∞

Jewell pulled on her gray sweat pants and over-sized t-shirt for bed. It was cold in Port Eastlyn, a town on the edge of the continent with the west side surrounded by water. The Victorian apartment with chintzy insulation and poorly-sealed windows stayed chilly. Besides, sexy attire was not a bedtime requirement these days.

Josh was already in bed reading when Jewell climbed in.

"Ready for lights out?" he asked.

"Sure," Jewell said with a deep sigh.

She lay close enough to welcome the warmth of his body. She remembered how physical their relationship had been in the early days after the fateful walk home from the movie theater and their first kiss.

"Are you asleep?" he asked.

"No."

"What's on your mind?"

The stillness of the night promoted an air of nostalgia. "I was thinking about us," she said.

"Us?"

"Yes, about the early days."

"You mean when you passed up all the other available seats to move in on the irresistible redhead in the front row?"

"Ha ha. No, my thoughts were more on the next year, on the porch."

"Ah, the first kiss when my skillful kissing served to overwhelm. I had tons of practice."

"Sure, you did, the back of your hand, your mirror, your pillow."

"Busted. Those were great days, though. Remember how we'd rush to your house, your bedroom, when we knew the Thompsons would be working late at the college?"

"Yeah, we discovered all types of things with our clothes heaped on the floor. Fun things I might add. So much fun we stole away every time we could."

"You were my first and my only. I can't imagine being with anyone else."

"Of course. Same here. Why did you feel the need to state the obvious?"

"I don't know, insecurity these days, I guess," Josh said. "What happened to us and the passion?"

"It fizzles with every couple. It's normal."

"I don't believe it goes away altogether. I think the frequency lessens, but it doesn't go away. I can't remember the last time."

Jewell remembered the last time. It had been the day of her graduation from the master's program. She flew high, full of optimism. She had landed the job at Oliver and Timpleton, a dream job as an associate. Her internship served her well. The commute between college and the lab paid off.

They made passionate love the afternoon before her graduation ceremony. It had been the first time in months, many months. She had quit counting. But beaming with emotion, they broke the celibate streak.

Their afternoon lovemaking had sparked hope for a full recovery of their love life. But as she lay in the bliss, wet from perspiration and slowing her breathing, those hopes were squelched. Josh announced he didn't feel up to going to her graduation or the after-party. She jumped to her feet, grabbed her clothes and stormed out of the bedroom. This signified their last time.

To Jewell, this had constituted a juncture in their relationship leaving them with a deep friendship and broken remnants of a romance. Still, she continued to refer to him as her boyfriend, out of habit she supposed, or because they had molded themselves into a marriage of sorts.

If Josh reserved so little regard for their last time, she would offer no words to enlighten him on the subject. The room fell silent and she continued to rifle through her memories.

They had completed their high school requirements a year early and had gone straight from high school to college together. With Jewell's intelligence, she had the ability to leave high school earlier, but she didn't want to attend college without Josh. Her last foster parents being educators helped her obtain scholarships for the University of Washington. The pair coalesced finding little need to seek other friendships.

Josh had always been a homebody, but Jewell remembered a pivotal turn their senior year at the university.

He wanted to stay at her apartment more and more. He showed no interest in the activities they had once enjoyed. He preferred to stay in to watch movies in the apartment rather than the theater.

He had also delegated the shopping and outside errands to Jewell. In hindsight, she pinpointed the time frame as the beginning of his crippling phobia.

Earlier, upon completion of their undergraduate degrees, he had ditched the plan of them both pursuing master's degrees and became a freelance writer, a career he could run from home.

By the time they had found their current apartment, Josh was close to shut-in status. She had managed to persuade him, several times, to visit doctors. The various treatments would work for a period of time and then Josh would tire of the desensitization or counseling modalities. In addition, he would eventually despise the side effects of each medication and stop taking them. He quit trying any type of treatment and accepted his fate of being closed in. Never, as far as Jewell could discern, had he considered what a burden it placed upon her.

Exhausted from reminiscing, Jewell's mind finally quieted. She heard the silence and lay in the deafening hush.

The quiet was broken as Josh whispered, "Blondie, I'll try your drug."

Four

A Clearly Indecisive Decision

"Are you staying late tonight?" Erin asked Jewell.

"For a little bit. I need to interpret mounds of data." She lied.

"Ok, see you tomorrow."

Jewell waited until the lab was empty. She knew the security staff's schedule and the location of the cameras.

Any genius with a computer and time on her hands is bound to test her hacking skills. Jewell hacked for entertainment and for the sheer joy of possessing the ability, nothing more. She promised herself never to use the skills for harm or unlawful activities, yet she sat poised to manipulate the inventory of drug supply along with the checks and balances in place to catch any manipulations. She took only a two-week supply of the medication for Josh to try. Her chest tightened. She counted on the ends justifying the means. She was helping Josh.

∞∞∞

Josh took the experimental drug for two weeks. He didn't report any side effects and agreed to continue taking it. Jewell increased his dosage and monitored him.

After a month on the drug, two weeks on the higher dose, Josh was able to walk out of the apartment and down the stairs into the yard. He only attempted this when Jewell accompanied him.

"Howdy neighbors," called Frank from the first-floor porch. Romeo took a break from chasing squirrels to hop onto the porch when he heard Frank.

Frank bent to pet the zealous Romeo. "We were just trying to figure out the last time we saw you, Josh. Ages we figured. Karyn and I are amazed at your commitment to stay in and write. I don't have the discipline."

"Well, Jewell's letting me take a break today."

They all laughed. Jewell and Josh exchanged a glance.

Josh continued to improve until he successfully walked around the block and then as far as the nearest store. Once he had enough courage to make the trip alone, he was excited to report the progress to Jewell.

She was so thrilled with Josh's progress, the next week at work she blurted to Erin before thinking, "You would be surprised at Josh and how much he's improved. He can go outside and walk around the block on his own."

"Oh, I didn't know you convinced him to go to a doctor again. You didn't tell me he agreed to another one and to start treatment."

Jewell bit her lip when she realized she said too much. "I didn't tell you? I could have sworn I did. Yes, he's going to someone and doing better."

"Awesome. What's he on now? Who's he seeing?"

"Oh gosh, I forgot about a conference call." Jewell fled to her office.

"Stupid, stupid, stupid," she said under her breath as she paced the floor of her office. "I know better. Don't tell people anything personal."

∞∞∞

Jewell entered the apartment. Other than Romeo running to her, the apartment hung silent. She looked around for Josh and found him sitting at the kitchen table with a paper in his hand, staring at her.

"What's wrong? What is it?" she asked.

"You got a fax."

"A fax?"

"Yeah, you know, printed information sent electronically over phone lines."

"I understand what a fax is. What is the faxed document you're holding?"

"Seems to be a job offer for you. About as far away from here as one can stretch, Southbridge, Florida."

Jewell couldn't believe she had forgotten to switch the fax option from the printer to her cell phone. She also couldn't believe the hospital still sent faxes.

"Oh, I was fantasizing the way I do," Jewell said, her voice a little shaky. "On the Internet, about moving somewhere and starting a new adventure. I suppose I accidentally hit 'send.' How could I leave?"

"Why not? I think you should. I feel the longing you carry around inside for a different life. I'm fine now. But, I'm curious; the place with the offer isn't a pharmaceutical company."

"I don't want to run projects anymore. I want to perform hands-on research again. This is a center for addiction within a major health system where they research effective treatments. I could contribute to people seeking relief from addiction. No one helped my mom, but maybe I can help someone else's mom so they don't run away from their kids. Besides, the hours aren't as demanding and I want a life outside of work."

Her eyes flashed to Josh and she quickly recanted. "I mean a more active life outside of work."

"No, I get it. It can't be fun stuck here with me." He stood up and took her hands. "Seriously, I will be fine now. I can go out. I'm independent again. My lady, I set you free." He made a sweeping motion with his arm as if opening a door followed by a bow.

"You can come with me," Jewell cried out with a tear in her eye.

"You know I can't. I'm just now able to progress out a little bit. Hell, this is the town I was born and raised in and it took medication and baby steps to push me out. I can't start all this deconditioning in a strange environment. I'd never adjust. Besides, I don't think the brief walks I'm able to take now compare to the plans you envision. I would still hold you back. Jewell, accept the offer."

With a stream of tears, she stepped into his open arms as he wrapped them around her in one of his teddy-bear hugs. She lost control and sobbed.

∞∞∞

Jewell went to bed with the excitement of a new life ahead but awoke in the morning with second thoughts.

She lay next to Josh. "Are you awake?"

"I am."

"I can't do it."

"Do what?"

"Move. Leave you."

"You can." He partially sat up in bed and leaned on his forearm to face her. "You are the bravest person I've ever met. You went through all of those foster homes. Sure, my grandmother raised me, not the most ideal situation given her health and age, but you went through way more and never broke down. You are so strong. You're my hero and always have been."

"No, you're my hero."

"Jewell, we can't deny the love we hold for one another and always will. We've been joined at the hip since we were kids. It doesn't mean we belong together for the rest of our lives though. We want different things. I witnessed how you pass the hours on your computer living vicariously through others. You put on a brave face, but you're hurting. And you're bored and lonely. You need to do this for yourself. Plus, I don't want to be pushed into doing things I don't want to do nor command the ability to do. I live with guilt all the time for holding you back."

"Maybe?" she replied.

"Only one major question."

"What?"

"Who gets Romeo?"

∞∞∞

Over the course of the next few weeks, Jewell made preparations for her move. She accepted the job in Southbridge and submitted her resignation at Oliver and Timpelton.

She searched online and found a charming house to rent in downtown Southbridge. She sent the deposit sight unseen.

Another part of Jewell's preparation included devising a plan to procure Josh enough drug supply to last until it reached FDA approval. She anticipated a short period. Once it was marketed, he would be forced to obtain the drug through a doctor. This prospect pleased Jewell because, in her opinion, he had needed regular monitoring for some time anyway.

On her last day at Oliver and Timpelton, she had lunch with Erin in the cafeteria per Erin's request. Erin attempted to engage

Jewell in her critical banter of the other employees and their various cliques, but Jewell refused to participate. She hoped to meet people in her new life similar to those in the cafeteria. She viewed them as social people too busy having fun to sit and critique others. She watched how they were engrossed in conversation and laughter not scanning the cafeteria to spot someone to criticize.

"Erin, instead of talking about the others today, why don't you tell me what you're going to do when I'm gone? I'm worried about you."

"I'll be alright. You're not much fun lately anyway."

"I'm sorry. I don't feel the same as I did when I started here. I don't think the others are all bad anymore."

"Fine, I'm finished eating." Erin stormed out of the cafeteria.

At the end of the workday, Jewell went to Erin's cubical, but she had gone for the day. Jewell laid the plant and card she had gotten for her next to her computer. As she turned to exit the cubical, a photo of her and Erin pinned to the wall caught her eye. She touched it lightly.

Jewell's desk contents were loaded into a box. The walls were never adorned with family photos or purposeless decor so it was easy to wrap up. She picked up the box to leave when she saw Taylor leaning in her doorway.

"Oh, hi," Jewell said, surprised to see her there.

"I wanted to wish you luck in your new endeavors. I hope you find what you're looking for."

"Um, thanks."

Jewell left, a little puzzled by Taylor's visit.

Five

A Drive of Transformative Proportions

On the fourth day of Jewell's exodus, the Florida sun, at its highest point of the day, scorched the inside of her Beetle bug like the intense heat of a Bunsen burner. Pools of sweat gathered under her thin legs, yet she hesitated to put the convertible top up. Instead, she basked in the blissfulness of too much sun helping her shed the memories of a long northwest winter. The prospect of her pale Washington skin burning, despite a generous slathering of sunscreen, bore no weight in her decision to keep the top down.

She thought of how this move almost didn't happen. On the day she had been scheduled to leave, she sat in their upstairs apartment questioning her resolve.

"Jewell!" Josh had called across the kitchen table and startled her the morning of her breakaway, causing her to splatter lukewarm coffee over her hand. "You've been staring at your cup the way you do when you're stressed. We've been over this, I'll be fine. Your drug is helping me. I can go out again."

"But you'll be alone and what about your dosage and your

supply?"

"Jewell, it's time," his words short and nudging. They had reached the door, but he showed no interest in walking her to the already-packed car. He pulled her into his body with a fury allowing her to capture his warm and familiar closeness once more.

His embrace tied her stomach into knots and planted a lump in her throat. Her tears welled and gushed. As she withdrew from his hold, she turned the doorknob and stepped onto the porch.

She turned back to survey him and witnessed a lost man as he raised his hand in a stilted wave and mouthed the words, "Take care, Blondie".

She chuckled as she recalled his words of advice about making friends, "And babe, try not to talk all 'sciency' to them. It scares people off."

She shook off her retrospection, pulled in a deep breath, devoured the scent of salty air, then blew it out slowly. She turned to her travel companion and called over the wind and road noise, "Oh, Romeo, we are doing the right thing. We'll get out and really live here. We'll make friends and do things outside of our four walls."

Romeo whined, out of courtesy, she supposed. He turned to her briefly then carried on with the business of sticking his snout out the window of his car carrier, his long ears flapping in the wind.

They came to a stop on the drawbridge carrying them into the oldest city in North America. It was made of thick poured concrete and held two stone horses majestically perched on each end. The bridge spanned the Intracoastal Waterway. Sails of bright white on crystal blue water sparkled decorating the waterway like a Monet painting. It took her breath away.

"We'll call this the Stallion Bridge, Romeo."

She stretched her arm to the back seat and through the window of his carrier so she could sink her fingers in his curls.

Locating their house proved as breezy as the last leg of the trip. She recognized it from the Internet photos. The cottage-style home with its yellow shingles and white gingerbread trim sat nonchalantly on the corner lot as to not rile a fuss in a town frozen in the sixteenth century.

Romeo pounced in the fenced front yard to confront a squirrel. He seemed happy to bound on solid ground once more.

Jewell unloaded the bug and chose to ignore the piles of caramel wrappers on the floor. The degree of her stress directly correlated to the measurement of candy waste.

She entered through the arbor and followed the long sidewalk leading to the front door. Inside, the kitchen contained boxes of her belongings courtesy of the property manager meeting the movers on her behalf. She prided herself on being thrifty, despite her healthy financial status, but scratched her head as she realized after twenty-seven years of life her treasures fit into a whopping thirty-some boxes. Fortunate for Jewell, it was a furnished rental.

She called Romeo to introduce him to their new home. It was a small home with the front door opening into the meager yet inviting kitchen. The interior colors were bright white and light blue. A recent cleaning blasted the air with a fresh lemony scent. Jewell deposited her keys on the island separating the kitchen and living room.

The layout was an open floor plan with the living room and sliding doors visible straight ahead leading to a back patio and another fenced yard. Off the living room, there were two small bedrooms and a blue ceramic-tiled bathroom in between.

The words bright and cheery came to mind as she scanned

the mermaid-themed decor throughout. The curvaceous sirens poised on predictable yet endearing signs read: "Mermaid Kisses and Starfish Wishes" and "Sea Hag [noun]: Mermaid before Coffee". Jewell decided she liked this whimsical house and it made her smile.

She thought of how this was the first time she had a home to herself and those thoughts reminded her she was overdue for her daily call to Josh.

"Hi, Jewell."

She figured her image popped up on his phone as it rang; the picture he had taken when she crossed her eyes and stuck her tongue out at him. The expression wasn't meant to be immortalized. She had begged him to delete it.

"We're here. At the new house."

"Oh good, I was worried about you two. How did Mr. Montague do with the trip?"

"Okay, but I think he's glad we're out of the car. How are you? And I mean the truth."

"I'm fine. I told you I would be," he said, curtly.

"Are you mad at me?"

"No, I'm fine."

"Well, anyway, remember to keep the pills in the airtight containers in the dresser drawer. You need to keep the light exposure down."

"I get it, I get it. Let's count, you told me once, twice, oh yeah and then again."

"Very funny, I want to make sure they last."

"What's it like there?" he asked more subdued, causing Jewell to question his level of interest.

"So far it looks like the Internet photos. Not like you spent much time looking at them with me, but the town is fascinating and the house..." Jewell curbed her enthusiasm, "the house is pretty cute."

"Good. I'm in the middle of an article so can I talk to you tomorrow? Or, if you're busy, you can text."

"Okay? Bye. Love you."

"Love you too."

She thought what an odd conversation. He had declared his support for her move, but now she wondered.

Jewell's tolerance for domesticity was exhausted after she unpacked enough boxes and suitcases to survive a couple of days. She snatched Romeo's leash and set out to explore their new town pleased with her decision to rent downtown.

Six

A Sign Sprouts from the Sidewalk

J ewell needed to plot the drive to the research building in
the hospital since she would start her new job in a few
weeks. But first, her interest lay in the Spanish-influenced
downtown with ancient stone buildings founded on cobblestone
roads laid out like a patchwork quilt with each square a coffee
shop, quaint boutique, restaurant or bed and breakfast.

A horse-drawn buggy shot by with a whoosh carrying chat-
tering passengers. The propped open shop doors delivered
an inviting communal milieu and Jewell made a game out of
searching these close to identical buildings for the subtle nuances
setting them apart. Friendly people leisurely passed.

She was full of excitement and anticipation of a new life. She
remembered the best spring of her life, her sophomore year in
high school when her emotions came to life and she held hope
for the future.

No vehicles were permitted to travel inside the blocks, only the
outer perimeter. The lack of modern vehicles further cemented
the sixteenth-century perception inside the grid.

As she rounded one of the many intertwining corners, a wooden sign begged her attention. Hanging on a wrought-iron post, the thing blended so well with its surroundings, she imagined it had sprouted from the pavement of its own volition centuries ago like a plant or small tree. Three lines adorned it:

The Sacred Veil Studio
Owner/Instructor: Margaret M. Porter
AKA "Maggie of the Silk Veil"

Bellydance? She wondered from the studio name. Four stone steps led to the door of a basement studio and an undeniable force summoned her down.

Jewell pushed the door open and checked side to side. The lack of response prompted her to creep in a little further, convinced she had stepped into a genie's bottle. Scarves of plum, gold, and the deepest fuchsia draped the walls.

Cushions and pillows were placed on the floor to provide seating. The pillows sported beads glistening in the soft lamplight like the sequins of an overdone prom dress.

The lack of sunlight in the basement bestowed a warm glow over the entire room. Painted Egyptian hieroglyphics peppered the floor. Mirrors covered the entire wall to her right and granted the room an appearance of vastness.

She was jarred from her trance by the sound of clicking buttons and groans. A purposeful glance in the mirror this time exposed a woman in the corner fidgeting with a remote control and aiming it at a music player. Her engrossment in the task at hand rendered her oblivious to Jewell's presence.

"Hello?" Jewell said with reservation.

"This dang thing, I cain't never get anything to work in this forsaken building."

She stood and revealed herself to be a tall graceful woman, oddly showing no signs of alarm from Jewell's unannounced presence in her studio. Jewell was thrown by the contrast of the woman's sophisticated air and her strong southern accent. They didn't match.

She was a stunning older woman maybe in her mid-fifties. Her glossy hair, white on the top, tapered into the gray of stainless steel to create the perfect reflective backdrop for her creamy complexion and piercing blue eyes to radiate. She was exquisite. Her long, lean legs marked her as a dancer, someone who had danced her whole life.

"Let me try," Jewell said and managed to persuade the machine to play the woman's selection. "What's that?"

"Tabla First Solo. Working on choreography for one of my troupes. I'm Maggie Porter." She stretched her right hand toward Jewell.

"I'm Jewell Caldwell." Jewell accepted Maggie's right hand.

"Are you from around here?"

"No, I'm from Washington State."

"Aw, I love Standard Poodles." Maggie went for Romeo's puffy head. "What brings y'all so far besides the beach, weather, and charm?" She provided a deep belly laugh hardier than Jewell suspected the occasion required.

"My employment. I'm a scientist, a researcher. I needed a change in my life and explored different areas on the Internet. Thanks to the reviews and virtual reality videos, I fell in love with the area and knew I wanted to live here."

"Are you here for the bellydance lessons?"

"Huh? Oh, right. No."

"Why ever not?"

"I've never danced before. I'm not much of a physical person. I'm more of a book/computer worm."

Maggie laughed again. "You'll do fine. My beginner's class already started. They are two weeks in now for the second time. The way it works, the students repeat the basic class twice before they move on to the advanced class."

"But." Maggie's eyes shot from Jewell's head to her toes, "There's not another group of newbies for you to join so maybe I could catch you up enough."

Maggie stroked her chin all the while looking to the ceiling. "I'll tell you what, come back on Wednesday at five p.m. That'll give us an hour to go over the basics and catch you up somewhat before the rest of your class arrives."

The rest of her class? She would meet new people, a revelation Jewell found both thrilling and terrifying.

"Okay," Jewell agreed, to her own surprise. She turned for the door, but Maggie stopped her.

"Wait, what are you doing right now? Can you stay for a bit? I was fixin' to work on choreo, but I can show you some basics. I'll also give you a link to my videos giving you time to practice before class."

"Sure." The prospect of anything other than unpacking appealed to Jewell.

Maggie directed Jewell to the wall of mirrors and positioned her to face it. She handed her a scarf with silver and blue swirls and coins dangling from the bottom. Maggie tied one to her own hips and Jewell copied her tying the scarf low around her hips.

"First, you need to be in proper bellydance stance." Maggie stood at her side to assist. "Kick off your shoes. Bellydance is an organic dance and the moves are grounded and connected. You need to allow the earthiness to seep in."

"Okay, feet flat on the floor, knees bent slightly, chest lifted, tuck your pelvis, find your core and engage those muscles." Maggie formed her hands into fists and placed them on her own abs to demonstrate.

"Let's clear our minds. Follow me."

They stretched, bending and twisting to the drum beats as Maggie called above the music to emphasize each beat for Jewell's benefit, "DOOM DOOM tekka tekka DOOM DOOM tek."

They launched into moves Maggie identified as hip bumps, hip lifts and drops. She showed her hip circles, both large and small, using the face of a clock as reference. She described how to isolate muscle groups, but told her it would take time to feel it and identify the desired muscles.

Jewell mimicked Maggie to the best of her ability as the silver coins dripped from the bottom of the scarf and clanked around her thighs.

The music, the instruction, and the hip scarf catapulted her to girlhood dreams of being a dancer.

The pair continued with the hip circles to the right, and then reversed to the left, and then half-circles to the front which Maggie called crescents.

As they danced, Jewell's pelvis warmed from the targeted supply of blood and filled her with a burst of eroticism. These provoking sensations flooded her as she performed the foreign moves, reminding her of past arousals. She wondered why a woman of her young age gave up on these feelings as if they would never come again.

∞∞∞

Jewell spent the next two days, after meeting Maggie, exploring her new town and practicing to Maggie's videos. Not being scheduled to start work for a few weeks afforded plenty of time for practice and exploration.

In fact, Jewell studied the bellydance videos with the fervor of an overachieving student, in part, driven by fear of scrutiny from her fellow students. So for two days, she planted herself in front of her living room TV where she streamed the videos and continued to drill the hip moves Maggie had shown her along with the additional shimmies and hip slides, to all of which she grew accustomed, but in no way mastered.

She moved on to chest isolations with similar lifts and drops, circles and slides. She could attest with complete certainty her chest had never before moved in any of these directions. All her muscles echoed the sentiment. Next, she practiced snake-like arm movements, holding her arms out to the sides until they throbbed.

Seven

A Highly Anticipated Class

⁓ ❧❧ ⁓

On the evening of the highly anticipate class, Jewell told Romeo she had to leave but would be back soon. She smiled at his cuteness as he cocked his head in what she assumed was an attempt to understand her.

Jewell's rental house was on one side of town and the studio on the opposite. She was enjoying the scenery of her daily walks and becoming familiar with the town.

When she reached the studio, Maggie greeted her enthusiastically.

"I'm glad you decided to come back. Not all do. How was the practicing?"

"I diligently practiced and used muscles I didn't know I had. Trust me, they're screaming at me."

"Ha, does it hurt to laugh?"

Jewell scrunched her eyebrows and turned the left corner of her mouth down trying to think of the last time she genuinely laughed. There had been the time in the yard when she and Josh faked a laugh for their neighbor, Frank's, benefit. They were happy for him to believe Josh's work was responsible for his seclusion. But, it had been some time since she belted out a true laugh.

"Let's evaluate your progress."

Maggie positioned Jewell in front of the mirror as Jewell finished tying the hip scarf she had borrowed from Maggie.

"Remember the stance?" Maggie asked.

"I think so." Jewell assumed what she thought was the position. Maggie found it necessary to tweak her stance.

Despite her diligent practice, she feared her lack of coordination would show as she called rebelling muscles into action. The following forty-five minutes, the pair drilled the moves to music, which helped Jewell settle into a comfortable rhythm.

Her intense concentration was broken by the other students who filled the room. She thought how familiar they seemed with one another by their ease of conversation and relaxed manner. They busied themselves as they laid their belongings on the entry bench, slid their shoes off and donned hip scarves.

"Everybody, this is Jewel," Maggie said.

The students stopped their activities and turned to Maggie and Jewell. Jewell counted six students who from first glance stood out as significantly diverse in age and style. Paired off two by two, Maggie's introduction interrupted their friendly chatter.

She introduced the first pair as Della Rae, a vibrant woman likely in her mid-forties, and Sherry, a contrastingly plain woman appearing to be in her late-thirties.

Della Rae provided a boisterous "Welcome!" with a spirited Southern accent. Jewell pegged her for a "How's your mama?" and "Bless your heart" wielding Southern lady who served up iced tea sweeter than her smile.

Sherry offered a shy smile.

"This is Nicci and Candi." Maggie gestured towards the tall woman appearing to be in her late-thirties and the curvy blonde surely in her early-thirties.

"Hi," Candi said, half-heartedly, her eyes zipping up and down Jewell.

"I don't understand," Nicci said, through pursed lips looking past Jewell and offering no greeting. "How can she start in the middle of our classes? How is she going to catch up? We're not going to be forced to slow down, are we?"

Jewell's cheeks flushed.

Maggie said, "Let me worry about how to conduct my class, thank you."

Nicci gave a quick, "Humph."

"And lastly, this is Becca and Z," Maggie concluded.

Jewell caught Maggie's eye-roll over the announcement of Z's name.

Z, with her abundant piercings and tattoos, gave an animated wave and smile. She appeared to be close to Jewell's age and Jewell liked her enthusiasm.

Becca also appeared close to Jewell in age. She smiled a warm smile and walked toward Jewell wrapping her arms around her.

Jewell regretted how she stiffened to Becca's hug.

The students were gathered around Maggie who described the night's agenda when a woman burst through the door in haste. Jewell would guess this woman to be in her late-thirties, a little chunky with disheveled hair. She hopped across the floor on one foot while prying a shoe off the other. Her bag fell to the floor and sloshed its contents of matchbox cars, candy wrappers, new and used tissues, wadded receipts and tampons.

"Sorry I'm late," she said, winded. "The kids were wound up."

"And this is Gabby. She's got twelve kids or something," Maggie said with a shudder and dismissive wave of her hand. "Gabby, this is our new student, Jewell."

"I have four; only FOUR," Gabby said in a loud yet jovial voice. "Welcome, Jewell."

"Four, twelve, what's the difference?" Maggie said.

Jewell guessed her instructor had none of her own.

The students filled the area in front of the mirror. Jewell was drawn to Becca and stood next to her. She possessed an overt sweetness about her signaling she would never hurt anyone.

The class was poised to begin lessons when an intrusive security alarm with alternating bellows, whistles, and high-pierced screeches caused all but Maggie to cover their ears.

"Here we go again, girls!" Maggie struggled to turn off the racket by pressing the keypad in the box on the wall.

Becca leaned over and whispered to Jewell, "This goes off every Wednesday at 6:10 p.m. and no one else is in the building but us. Maggie thinks a ghost triggers the alarm."

Jewell turned to Becca wide-eyed.

"Yep, she reports strange happenings all the time such as items moved and electronics not working," Becca said.

The offensive noise was silenced after Maggie satisfied the alarm with keypunches allowing the class to commence.

They went through more drills. Some similar and some new moves, all danced to primal rhythms. Jewell watched in the mirror and judged the other students more natural.

Maggie spouted deafening commands over the drum beats. One command Jewell couldn't quite grasp as she tried to decipher, "Ford back Ford. Ford back Ford."

Jewell leaned toward Becca and whispered, "What is it about a Ford?"

"Ha, no, 'forward back forward,'" Becca said with a giggle. "Her accent trips me up too. Watch, we twist the ball of our foot forward in front of us and then backward behind us and then forward again."

The time flew and class ended, filling Jewel with dread at the thought of spending another week in solitude until the next class. She was lonely enough in Washington, but at least she had Josh.

Becca praised her for keeping up with the class and Della Rae sprinted to her side to convey the same. Soon, Sherry, Z, and Gabby delivered similar appraisals.

While the group grabbed their belongings to exit, another group of women entered the studio. Some smiled and spoke to the beginner students, while others ignored them.

Jewell frowned as she followed her class out of the studio.

When she reached the door, Becca made a 180-degree turn to face her. "We all go out for coffee afterward. Do you want to come?"

Jewell was thrilled at the invitation, but didn't want to sound too eager. She decided to respond with an air of composure and pretended to analyze a schedule on her phone. "Sure, I can go."

∞∞∞

Rhita's Daily Perks was only two blocks from the studio so the group walked. On the way, Becca lagged behind to walk with Jewell. She was taller than Jewell, but with a similar petite frame. She had long light-brown wavy hair. Her loose top draped to one side revealing a slender shoulder.

"I grew up near here, at Crescent Beach. I'm a barista temporarily, but I think I want to be an interior designer someday. I'm not sure yet. What about you? Are you from around here?"

"No, I recently moved from a small port town in Washington. I moved for a new position."

"Oh wow, what do you do?"

"I'm a researcher, a scientist."

"Whoa. I didn't even finish college. I got bored. Good for you."

There was a pause in the conversation until Becca asked in a sing-song manner, "Are you married, or is there a boyfriend?"

Jewell listened to the click-clack of her sandals on the cobblestones as she weighed her answer. She and Josh had never married and she really couldn't call him her boyfriend any longer. The words had not been spoken, but they were for all practical purposes, broken up.

"No, I'm not married and no boyfriend. I live with my pet, Romeo."

"What type of pet?"

"A standard poodle."

"Aw, I want to meet him. And don't worry about not having a boyfriend. You'll meet someone at work. Or…" Becca trailed off. "I can't imagine. I'm never without a boyfriend. I could count my long-term boyfriends on one hand, but there always seems to be one to fill the role for short stints. I like someone at work now, but I think he's oblivious at this point. He works here too."

They reached the steps of the coffee shop. "This is where I work as a barista."

Jewell had passed Rhita's on her explorations and intended to go inside several times, but never made it. As they entered the shop, the mingling scents of cookies and vanilla flooded her senses and reminded her of the first foster mom. A barrage of good and bad memories from her childhood lurked in her mind, but the memories of her first foster mother were touching ones.

She remembered how the sweet lady, who baked goodies even sweeter, would wrap her in a blanket and rock her to sleep. She sang to Jewell and smelled of cookies and vanilla. She had been three years old and her brother Nathanael, six. It was the only foster home they had been able to stay in together, the fragile family unit ripped apart by the nurturing lady's husband no longer wanting kids hanging around, stealing his wife's attention. Afterward, the constant move from family to family and home to home became commonplace.

The unfinished hardwood floor of the coffee shop creaked like the floor in the Washington apartment. In line, Jewel read the display of clever signs such as: "Behind Every Successful Person is a Substantial Amount of Coffee" and "A Yawn is a Silent Scream for Coffee."

She scanned the room and observed how every eye in the shop stopped at Candi, both men and women alike. With her long straight blonde hair, her tall curvy body and the uncanny ability to strike a sensual pose in an instant, Candi commanded attention.

"This happens everywhere we go, as if she minds," Becca whispered as they moved through the line behind the others. "She works at one of those high-end department-store cosmetic counters at the mall. The kind where the salespeople wear lab coats. But we all think she just wants to land a rich husband."

"Hello, Becca," a voice called from behind the coffee shop counter.

"Hi, Renaldo," she called back.

Jewell analyzed Becca's flushed cheeks and how she stood on her toes to wave back fervidly. She turned to Jewel, her confession unnecessary, "He's the one. The one I like."

Renaldo was cute, with his black wild-wispy hair, facial stubble, green eyes, and a devilish grin.

"He's so quiche," Jewell said, as she uncomfortably tried to interject the slang she had studied, dialect she read someone her age should be using.

Becca drew back to view her, "Wait, what?" she said with a slack-jawed expression.

"Oh, nothing. He's hot," Jewell said. "What should I order?"

"I recommend you come back when I'm working." Becca chuckled. "Do you like yours sweet?"

"I do."

"You should order the White Chocolate Macadamia Nut. By the way, what's your number?" Becca asked, poised to press the buttons on her phone.

Jewell recited her number as Becca committed it to her contacts.

"Say cheese." Becca snapped a picture of Jewell to add to her contact information. "I'll text you later so you'll have my number."

A small space with an intimate flare, the shop held tables situated close together. There was an inviting air to the place as cozy as hydrogen and oxygen. Most tables accommodated couples or small groups. There was one large table, a round one with eight seats sitting empty.

As the group headed for the round table, Jewell stayed close to Becca to assure a spot next to her. She was still a little intimidated by the group as she chartered new territory.

She glanced at the members spread around the table with the same ease they displayed in class. Each sat with her own ceramic mug of tea or coffee. Jewell lifted her cup of steaming brew to her lips and inhaled the bouquet of delicate white chocolate mixed with the earthy scent of nuts. She delighted in the warm sugary liquid as it rolled through her mouth and down her throat.

"This is all of us," Nicci informed in report-fashion. Jewell assumed the declaration was for her benefit.

"Maggie doesn't come because she has her advanced class following the beginner's class. You probably saw some of the..."

she paused, "well, let's just say some of the 'superior,'" she raised her fingers in air quotes, "students. And—"

"Lord above, no need to give the poor girl a sermon," Della Rae said.

"And, as I was saying," she flashed a glare at Della Rae, "Gabby doesn't come for coffee because, well, because of all those kids."

Nicci nodded in agreement with herself causing her dark tight curls to spring about her head. Her dark smooth skin reminded Jewell of creamy chocolate mousse and she noted what a beautiful woman Nicci was, wearing oversized dark-rimmed glasses and plum lipstick with a finesse few could pull off.

"The advanced class is also a performing troupe," Becca said.

"And we're so glad you joined our class, Jewell," Della Rae said with the most genuine smile.

"Thank you, I'm glad too. I think I'm going to be happy here in Southbridge."

"Oh, where are you from?" asked Sherry.

"Washington. The state of Washington, not D.C." Jewell deemed her answer enough.

The group deemed otherwise as they launched into a string of questions.

Sweat beaded on the back of her neck reminding her why she avoided groups.

"Why did you move?" asked Nicci.

"For a new job." Jewell measured her words.

"What do you do?" asked Z.

"I'm a researcher, a scientist."

"Wow. Impressive," said Della Rae.

"How does someone your age rise to such a level?" Nicci folded her arms and narrowed her eyes through her oversized glasses.

"I guess I was a science nerd in high school and college. I enjoy research and experiments."

"Brainiac," Candi said.

"What do you do for fun?" asked Sherry, the quiet one with a small stature and unassuming looks, one who could get lost in a group this size. She pushed the straight dishwater-blonde strings of hair behind her ears in a nervous fashion and awaited Jewell's answer.

"Not too much," Jewell said.

"So yeah, like, we really need to get you out more. Like who does that, stays in or whatever? Come on let's get you out," said Candi. She chanted "Girls' night, girls' night," only to stop abruptly. She spun to Jewell, "Wait, are you married?"

Heads snapped towards Jewell with such velocity she marveled how no one suffered whiplash.

She took a sip of coffee. It turned into a gulp as she looked around the table at the eager eyes upon her. She heard the hissing of steam from the espresso machine behind the table.

"I can't image she isn't or at least has a boyfriend as pretty as she is," Della Rae said to Sherry.

"I agree," Sherry said.

"Well, I think she should tell us," Candi said.

She decided it would be safest to remain evasive. "No, there's no one."

"No one?" asked Nicci raising her eyebrows.

"Well, except Romeo." She said, but failed to consider the group's oblivion to Romeo being a dog.

"Who is this Romeo?" asked Della Rae. "He sounds sexy."

"Oh Romeo, Romeo, wherefore art thou Romeo?" Z sang.

"Leave her alone," Becca said.

But to Jewell's surprise, she was relaxing. Maybe it was Becca's support or the way Z toyed, but in uncharacteristic fashion, she too became playful. "Well he's a big, dark and curly…" she held her breath.

The others waited, passing glares from one another.

"…standard poodle," she blurted.

She gave a real laugh for the first time in a long time, folding her arms over her abdomen to brace the aching muscles.

"Oh you," said Della Rae.

"Not funny," said Sherry.

"Owe, stop making me laugh, it hurts."

"You started it," Z said, giggling until she had tears.

"Y'all are going to make me pee my pants," Della Rae said.

"And now you have us too." Becca looped her arm through Jewell's.

Jewell marveled over the outgoing and comfortable manner Becca took with her, someone she had met only a little over an hour prior.

"So, how about our regular alarm again tonight?" asked Della Rae.

"You know, Maggie's, like, convinced a ghost is behind these things," Candi said.

"Exactly," said Becca, "the alarm goes off every Wednesday at exactly 6:10 p.m. and the alarm company has no idea why. Objects are constantly misplaced and you can hear the ever-so-faint sound of laughter and finger symbols so faint you think you might be hallucinating."

"Oh man, and what about the sudden random whiff of patchouli in the air," Sherry said.

"Remember the night we heard the howling through the duct system?" asked Della Rae.

"BOO!"

Everyone at the table jerked and turned to glare at Z. She had seized the opportunity to scare her classmates after returning from the bathroom. She bent over with a belly laugh.

"Oh, very funny Z," said Della Rae.

"Okay, I'm calling it a night," said Nicci.

"Me too," said Becca.

The group stood to leave.

A twinge of sadness struck Jewell as the group split. She was getting ready to leave when Becca called to her.

"I'll text you later."

∞∞∞

When Jewell arrived home, she walked Romeo and called Josh as they moseyed.

"How did your first class go?"

Josh was up to date with Jewell's life. They phoned almost daily and often texted throughout the day, finding it difficult to break the bond they had created over the last twelve years.

"It was great. I didn't make a fool of myself dancing."

"The thought never crossed my mind."

"And after class, we all went out for coffee." This time Jewell didn't try to curb her enthusiasm.

"It looks like you're closing in on the life you wanted, babe."

"I think so, but what about you?" A pang of guilt struck her.

"I'm great and guess what? I'm about eighty-five percent through the novel. Inspiration has struck."

"Awesome, so the medicine isn't interfering with your creativity this time?"

"What? Oh yeah, right. No, it doesn't seem to be this time."

"I'm exhausted. Can we talk tomorrow?"

"Sure. Good night. Love you."

"Good night. Me too."

Jewell found it awkward to climb into bed alone after being

50

accustomed to sleeping with Josh for so many years. She was lying in bed and rerunning her eventful day when her phone pinged.

She turned on the lamp to check her phone. A text message from an unknown phone number displayed.

Text: Hi, this is Becca. Now you have my number!

Seconds later, a picture uploaded.

Becca again: Now you can upload my pic and add it to your contact list.

Jewell: Thanks. What's your last name?

Becca: Steal. Want to practice bellydance some this Saturday.

Jewell was not used to such forwardness, but she wanted things to be different here. Maybe this is how it's done? She typed a response and hit "enter" before she had time to over analyze it.

Jewell: Okay, great.

Becca: Can we practice at your place? My family won't let you alone, with you being new and all.

Jewell: Sure. 132 St. Anthony Street. What time?

Becca: I'm scheduled to open Rhita's Saturday morning, but get off early so I could be there around 10:30 ish in the morning. Would that work?

Jewell: Perfect.

Becca: BTW, how about going to Chelsea's Diner after we practice?

Jewell: Yeah, I pass there and would love to try it.

Jewell found falling asleep difficult between the excitement of class, Rhita's, and now Becca coming to her house. She dared to think her dreams were starting to come true.

Eight

A Cowboy, a Farmer, and a Good–Looking Guy Walk into a Diner

S aturday morning at 10:30 a.m.

Becca texted: You up?

Jewell: I am!

Becca: OMW…and I'm bringing my famous French-pressed coffee.

Jewell: Yum. See you soon.

Becca: Leaving Rhita's now. Driving, so real soon.

As promised, Becca arrived moments later, with a thermos in hand.

Romeo accompanied Jewell to the door, his tail wagging.

"Aw, this must be Romeo," Becca cooed.

"Yes." Jewell started, but found Becca already on the floor with him, lifting the thermos to Jewell.

Romeo played, barking at Becca, as if conversing, so excited his tail wagged his whole body.

"Your house is adorbs."

"I'd show you around, but can you wait until I unpack?"

"Of course. I can help if you want."

"Thanks, but I'll get to it sometime."

Jewell retrieved two mugs from the cabinet. She had at least unpacked the box marked "Mugs and Wine Glasses". She poured the gourmet coffee from Becca's thermos and basked in the aroma of the dark liquid promising comfort and arousal.

She handed Becca her cup and offered cream and sugar.

"No thanks, mine is good like this. Why don't you try it black first?"

"Oh no, I never drink it without a healthy heaping of cream and sugar."

"One sip, and if you don't like it, you can add your old cream and sugar."

Jewell cautiously took a sip, her gaze fixed on Becca. She coached herself not to spit it out, regardless of how bad it tasted without her fixings. To her delight, Becca was right and she didn't need to "doctor up" Becca's specialty brew.

They decided to sit on the back patio. Jewell cupped her hands around the warm mug. Romeo coaxed the pair to throw his disc. He chased after it, wagging his tail in pure delight having two slaves at his command. The bright sun burned Jewell's bare knees.

The weekend hustle of cars and pedestrians was well underway. Becca sat on the cushy chair next to Jewell, her long legs curled on top of the cushion, twisted in a near pretzel formation.

Jewell studied with curiosity as Becca contorted her hair in various arrangements for no apparent reason, all the while chatting. Becca tossed her brown long locks behind her shoulder, then rolled them into some bun tied precariously on top of her head only to drop it back down, all in subconscious fashion.

"It must be nice to live alone. I still live with my parents and my younger sister, Brook. She's seventeen and quite the handful for mom and dad."

"I'm not sure living alone is better. And don't forget about Romeo. I'm not alone."

"Trust me, you're way better off."

"Where did you say you lived?"

"On the outskirts of town, at Crescent Beach."

"Oh, right. I was planning to visit the area but got busy with everything downtown offers, all within walking distance."

"Yeah, we are a little more spread out. How about your family? Are they in Washington?"

"No, my father died in a car accident when I was two years old. I don't remember him at all. Then our, I mean my, mother lef..." she stopped herself. "My mother died too."

"Oh no. I'm so sorry. When did your mother die?"

"When I was around three."

"Who took care of you? There was other family, right? Grandparents?"

"No, there was no one. I had to go to foster homes."

Becca slapped her hand over her mouth and shook her head. When she recovered enough to remove her hand, she said, "I can't fathom it. Was the foster family nice?"

Jewell figured Becca's only encounter with abandoned children and foster homes came from what she witnessed on TV, not from real life.

"There were families, plural. And some were nice and some not so warm, but I was never abused or anything. I had what I needed and threw myself into my studies."

"Gosh, no wonder you're so smart, and a scientist."

"Enough about me. Tell me about your parents."

"My Mom, Lynn, is a stay-at-home mom. She can't wait to meet you. Oh, I just realized, wait until she figures you no longer have your mom, she'll want to become your mother." Becca laughed. "My dad is a corporate lawyer. Boring." Becca sang the word boring.

"So, when we were walking to Rhita's the other night, you said you've never been in a significant relationship, right?" Jewell asked, at an attempt to hone the skill of friend-making.

"Well, actually I stand corrected, I had one, once. Andrew. It was in the eleventh grade. He went to a school near Southbridge Beach and I went to a private school in Crescent Beach; so there was the distance. The distance would be nothing for adults, but tough for high-school kids. We met at a Halloween party and dated the rest of the school year. He was my first, you know?"

"Uh-huh."

"I guess he broke my heart. Mom says I was living on a 'pink cloud.'" It was probably more of a bubble and he popped it. I thought we would be like my mom and dad, together forever. I pictured our house and our kids. I wrote my name with his last name on my notebooks, my bedazzled notebooks mind you."

They laughed and clanked their mugs.

"Only the last couple of months of the school year, he had been cheating with another cheerleader, of all things. Did I tell you I was a cheerleader?"

"No, but I can picture it."

"Well, this cheerleader was from his school. I ignored the signs. He called less and less and made excuses why we couldn't spend the entire weekend together as we always had, yada, yada."

"Aw, I'm sorry."

"Yeah, so I guess following Andrew, there has been one after another. I have the ability to attract them, no problem; I can't seem to keep them. I mean, I'm passionate and physical, but an antiquated notion seems to exist in guys where they love the pursuit but once caught, they're compelled to move on and catch another. I'm stuck in a vicious cycle."

"Oh, and along these lines, TADA!" Becca sounded. "I guess Renaldo and I are a thing now."

"Wow, a fast turn of events."

"I told you. Now, how about you? We've exhausted my love life. What about yours?" Becca wiggled to adjust in her seat.

"We better practice if we're going to go to lunch," Jewell said.

"Oh yeah, and we need to be at Chelsea's by one p.m."

"Why one p.m.?"

"Um, I'll be hungry by then," Becca answered.

"I usually stream Maggie's videos on my TV in the living room."

The pair took their places in front of the TV and drilled. Becca, the more seasoned student, assisted Jewell as needed.

When they completed practicing, they made their way to Chelsea's Diner.

It was outfitted in retro-style with a wraparound Formica bar and red plastic bar stools. Rows of booths lined the perimeter. Jewell pictured James Dean, Marilyn Monroe and Humphrey Bogart at the corner of the bar with Elvis behind it ready to provide service with a smile.

Jewell read the laminated menu.

"I always order the BLT and fries," Becca offered.

"Okay, me too."

"Oh, and their cherry Cokes are killer."

"Sold," Jewell replied and they laughed.

The pair enjoyed their food and more conversation about Becca's boyfriend escapades which Jewell found quite entertaining.

Then, the bite of sandwich Jewell had lifted halfway to her

mouth was discarded with a plunk when she caught sight of him entering the diner. He had the kind of knock-out looks with enough punch to cause a girl to chuck her sandwich; her interest in food perished. She tried to recall the last time she had eyed a cowboy, real or pretend. She had assumed they were extinct. He took off his hat liberating a rouge chestnut curl to topple onto his forehead. Patrons swiveled to gawk as he strutted the aisle between the bar stools and booths under the illusion of slow motion.

How anyone managed to maneuver so skillfully in painted-on jeans was a mystery. For that matter, she wondered how anyone managed to pour themselves into such tight pants to begin with, but was pleased he possessed the ability.

Her ogling eyes made it to his detailed leather boots as he approached their booth. He held his index finger over his mouth signaling to Jewell not to alert Becca who sat with her back to the dreamy one. He was about to tap Becca on the shoulder when she noticed Jewell's mesmerized stare and turned to discover the object of her hypnosis.

"Kage, oh Kage." Becca sprang from the booth to hug him. "Sit with us."

"Nah, you're almost done." His gaze locked with Jewell's.

"Come on, sit." Becca scooted over on the bench and patted her hand on space for him.

When he sat across from Jewell, she got a whiff of his earthy musky scent and she tried to drink it in without being caught.

"This is Kage, Jewell. He lives in Crescent Beach too. We went to school together."

"Where'd you go to school?" He asked.

Jewell begged her voice not to betray her.

"Oh, I'm not from here. I grew up in Washington, in Port

Eastlyn."

"Whoa, how'd you turn up here?"

"She came here for the bellydancing." Becca winked.

"I'd like to watch that," Kage said under his breath.

"No, actually I'm here for my employment. I'm a researcher and going to work at the Bernstein and Beck Center for Addiction. I start in ten days."

"It's in the hospital, isn't it?"

"It is."

"A researcher. Impressive."

"She's amazing," Becca said, "and beautiful too."

Jewell widened her eyes at Becca to beg her to stop.

"Kage is a rancher," Becca told Jewell.

"Farmer is more like it. We have a ranch, but it is more about the farming," Kage said.

That explains the getup and the tanned skin, Jewell thought.

"Well, rancher sounds sexier," Becca said.

"Farmer? Aren't you young to be a farmer?"

"Hey, I could ask you the same about being a researcher."

Jewell slapped her hand over her mouth and giggled, a gesture she didn't remember ever performing before. "Touche."

"No worries, we have a family farm and I realize you don't meet a rancher aka farmer every day, especially one so young, so good looking, so built..." He trailed off and laughed at himself.

Jewell wondered if everyone from Crescent Beach was as charming and outgoing as Becca and Kage. She imaged a mandatory interview with the mayor's staff to grant approval of all newcomers. The criteria: good looks and charisma.

"Um, Becca, I'm going to the Concert on the Greens next Saturday. The Totally Tubular band is playing around noon. Why don't you and whoever you're dating come with me? And don't try to tell me you're not dating anyone; you always are."

"Ha ha, very funny. But yes, I am dating someone." Becca stuck her tongue out.

Kage smiled a sly smile and winked at Jewell causing a reaction in her pelvic region similar to the reaction stirred by the new bellydance moves, only stronger. Hope for the revival of a vibrant love life burned bright.

"Anyway," Becca said, "his name is Renaldo and yes, I will ask him. Say, Jewell, why don't you come too?"

Jewell leaned back in the booth and crossed her arms, she drew out each word and nodded, "Well, isn't this all too convenient?"

"What? What do you mean?" Becca stumbled on her words and then conceded as it sank in how obvious she and Kage had been. "Well, what's the difference of how he ended up here today? Want to go?"

Jewell did want to go, even if she was being ambushed. She couldn't deny her attraction to the new cowboy but worried it was too soon to date. A twinge of guilt struck her as she pictured Josh in the apartment all alone and her already having way more fun than he, now this. Going to a concert on what was shaping up to be a double date? How could she? She visualized the cliche devil on one shoulder and angel on the other whispering their arguments into her ear. The devil and cowboy won.

"Okay, I'll go."

"Yay." Becca bounced on the cushy bench.

Kage smiled a sheepish grin.

∞∞∞

Jewell walked home brimming with excitement and energy. Energized to unpack and organize her new home, she dug in with inspired ambition. She had already had Becca over and was to have another certain person visiting soon.

59

She changed into clothes more suitable for unpacking and was ready to plunge in wearing comfortable jean shorts and a loose T-shirt. Her long blonde curls hung casually.

She lifted the heaviest box marked "Bedroom" and placed it on the coffee table. She remembered some of its contents and gazed at it for a few moments debating whether to open it or not.

She went to the kitchen and retrieved one of the many eclectic wine glasses she had placed in the glass-paneled cabinet to display their beauty through the glass. She poured a glass of Pinot Grigio from an open bottle in the fridge.

On the way back to the living room, she grabbed a knife and cut the tape sealing the box then sat cross-legged on the living room floor. She pulled out the photo album of her and Josh and ran her hand over the smooth brown cover not sure if she wanted to open it. She hugged it close to her chest. Maybe later, she thought and carefully set it aside.

The only other photo album in the box was the closest thing she had to a family album. It was of her and her brother Nathanael. They had always lived in the same small town, but she held no delusions of their closeness.

She realized they hadn't had the opportunity to bond the way other brothers and sisters raised in the same home did. Still, she took pictures at their twice-annual birthday meetings and saved them in a small album.

As she flipped through the pages, she thought of how they both were blessed with good looks, but in contrasting ways. Nathanael was endowed with dark bold features and she with fair coloring and delicate features.

She continued to reach into the box. Jewell took pride in how thrifty she could be in spite of her healthy salary and Josh's settlement. Not only the flea-market wine glasses but the antique clock she had kept on her bedside table. She remembered packing it in this box. She dug the clock from the bottom of the box and was beginning to unwrap it when a cold breeze swept over her followed by a boom from the bedroom.

Romeo startled to his feet. She grabbed the knife from the coffee table and slowly crept towards the bedroom. She flicked on the light. Romeo stood next to her.

"Is anyone in there? I have a gun," she lied, all the while plotting a quick exit. She discovered the mirror she had hung on the bedroom wall lying on the floor unbroken. She inspected the rest of the house, Romeo close by her side, to verify they were alone. She concluded the fault lay in her hammering skills.

She grabbed a pear from the kitchen island as she deduced the wine was going to her head. A glance at the time on her phone told her it was seven p.m.

She needed to check in with Josh. Afraid her voice may give away her excitement about the upcoming concert and her new cowboy friend, she decided to text.

The unpacking didn't wear her out enough to sleep. She lay in bed and reflected on her girlhood musings about dancers and ghosts, two things manifesting in her life.

Josh had believed they read all the same books, unaware Jewell reserved her own guilty-pleasure readings. She cherished her secrets as a hidden treasure locked securely in a box deep inside her. A treasure guarded even from Josh.

The books she had stashed between mattresses told stories of beautiful dancers with never-ending romances and intriguing heroines who explored paranormal happenings. Living from foster home to foster home afforded few privacies and this had been one she couldn't relinquish.

Although she had realized the reality of dance was left to the popular girls, like the cheerleader and her friend in the tight sweater from the back row. The two she had avoided the first day of class. Ashley and Steph were their names, but take one out and replace her with another from the myriad popular girls and no one would notice the swap.

As far as the paranormal went, how would it have come across for the genius student, grounded in scientific experiments, to be reading about ghosts, witches and extrasensory perception?

Nine

A Ghost Hunt

~⚬⚭⚬~

The next few days passed with Jewell practicing bellydance and continuing to explore downtown. A great deal of activity was required to distract her from thoughts of Kage, a futile undertaking at times. It proved an even more daunting task at bedtime. Saturday seemed like an eternity away.

On Wednesday, Jewell made her trek to the studio. The first place she passed was the Serenity Day Spa. On her initial visit to the spa, she found it a lavish yet serene place packed in a house scarcely larger than hers. Lavender and orange formed a congenial union and flooded her senses with a warm welcome as she opened the chiming door. She hadn't allowed herself such luxuries in Port Eastlyn, always focusing on Josh. Here, she enjoyed the freedom to indulge in massages and to linger in coffee shops, boutiques, and restaurants.

Jewell activated fresh enthusiasm for the vintage boutiques, taking a renewed interest in her appearance. She found herself changing her style a bit from casual, bordering on sloppy, into a more vintage style. The interest she had developed in her appearance the high-school year she turned Josh's head had fizzled after he had succumbed to his fears.

The next block contained the leash-free dog park she and Romeo had stumbled upon earlier in the week, allowing him to run free and expend the tightly wound energy, typical of a standard poodle. She had opened the gate their first visit, her fingers struggling to unhook his leash with his every thrust for freedom. Once she managed to unhinge the hook he barreled towards his new friend with barks and bounces.

He ran straight to another standard poodle. This one was red with bright white markings on his chest and on three of his paws. A woman with thick burgundy hair stood next to him. "Hi, I'm Tiffany."

"I'm Jewell and the excited one is Romeo."

Tiffany laughed. "He's a cutie, and sweet. This is Bentley."

"Who's your groomer? I'm searching for one and can tell you found a talented one. Bentley looks great."

"Thanks." She handed Jewell a business card with a phone number, email and a comedic picture of the cutest long-haired dog in rollers. The card further read:

Tiffany Robertson, Licensed Groomer
The Pampered Pet Spa
108 Maple Street, Southbridge, FL

"Yep, yours truly," the woman said.

∞∞∞

Jewell reached the studio for her second class and found Becca inside with her shoes off performing stretches. Candi and Nicci stood at the end of the bench in deep conversation and Della Rae sat on the bench removing her shoes.

"Well hey, Jewell, I'm happy to see you again," Della Rae said.

Maggie sat at her desk engrossed in some paperwork at the other end of the studio as Sherry and Z entered together.

Jewell dropped her backpack, slid off her shoes, and took her place next to Becca who hugged her and winked. "You'll be all caught up now after our practicing."

This time Jewell hugged her back.

Everyone was in their places ready for class when Gabby scurried in. The weekly alarm sounded on cue; however, this time it was accompanied with erratically flickering lights.

"What's with these lights? Did it look like a storm brewing outside?" Maggie asked.

The students shook their heads looking from one to another in agreement.

"It was sunny on my way in," Gabby said.

BAM! The dressing room door slammed shut.

Shrieks echoed throughout the studio. Della Rae clutched Jewell's arm. Maggie pointed to the studio door that had been left open.

"Gabby," Maggie reprimanded.

"Now listen, y'all," Maggie said, "the ghost is getting worse. It used to be items showing up across the room. Turning up in places I knew darn well I hadn't left them. It was kind of amusing. The alarm in your class and other happenings in the advanced class, but now things are out of hand. More strange moans are howling through the duct system and I swear drafts come from nowhere, blow by then pass quickly. I tell ya I'm afraid to be here by myself anymore which says a lot."

Jewell felt the hairs on her arms rise as she recalled the cold breeze at her house right before the mirror dropped.

"I think she's trying to grab my attention," Maggie said.

"Why do you think the ghost is a she?" Della Rae asked.

"Hmm, I don't know. I guess since this place is usually full of women, I just assumed. Does anyone have any knowledge of ghosts?"

The women looked from one to another.

"We can learn," Nicci said.

"Please do, and brief me. Now let's get to work."

The class carried on with lessons and Jewell followed along much more smoothly this week. Her confidence swelled and she caught Nicci watching her from the corner of her eye.

After the weekly post-class stretching, Z cheered. "Now we can go to Rhita's and talk about the ghost."

"I'm in," Gabby said.

"What?" Della Rae asked.

"Yeah, Kevin can keep the kids. I never get any excitement."

"Well, alright! Let's go," Becca said.

They decided to walk to Rhita's. Inside, they ordered their coffees and took their usual table left empty, Jewell figured, due to its size. The rest of the patrons were either alone or with one or two others.

"So, what can we like do about the ghost? I mean, have an exorcism or something?" Candi asked.

"First of all, there is no such thing as ghosts and second of all—" Nicci started but was interrupted by Della Rae.

"Then why did you say we could find out for Maggie?"

"To find out how to dispel this craziness. We will find logical explanations through researching the Internet and present the information to Maggie."

"I believe she's real," Z said.

"Me too," Gabby said.

"I agree. I say we try to figure out who she is and what she wants first," Della Rae said.

"What do you think, Jewell?" Sherry asked. "You're the scientist."

Jewell paused to give a thoughtful answer. It occurred to her they would expect a practical answer from a scientist despite her hidden fascination with the paranormal. "The existence of ghosts has not been disproved, so I say the existence of ghosts is possible."

"Humph." Nicci drew her laptop from her executive leather bag. "Alright, we'll do it your way, but I'm telling you, we'll discover what utter nonsense this is."

"Does anyone else think the haunting has increased since last week?" Sherry asked as Nicci worked to sign into the wifi.

The others nodded in agreement and slowly shifted their eyes towards Jewell, the new dynamic added in the past week.

Della Rae said, "Um, there's definitely an increase. We used to joke about it not really believing it was a ghost. It was a game. Maggie was the only one convinced. The happenings included the usual 6:10 p.m. alarm, missing objects, oh, and the electronics Maggie can never seem to work. We were used to all those, but now the flickering lights, door slamming and Maggie's reports of moans and drafts from nowhere."

"Someone..." Nicci nodded towards Gabby and cleared her throat, "...left the studio door open creating a vacuum."

"Okay, here we go," Nicci said. "There are so many sites; I can't discern which are legit. I use certain dot org sites for business research, but am not sure what to trust here."

"Read through some and we'll try to figure it out based on consistency."

"Yeah, go for it."

Nicci read her initial search results to the group, "There are several types of ghosts and they can take on various forms. The most common ones seen haunting are either family members or historical figures. They can make their presence known visibly, through noises, touch, or an odor such as perfume, herbs or tobacco, for example."

"Now, what a bunch of nonsense," Nicci said about her readings.

"Well, I'd say our ghost is noisy," Sherry said.

"But she can keep the touch stuff to herself," Z said.

"The visibility aspect." Jewell contemplated. "It would be helpful if we could capture an image, something to aid in identification."

Nicci argued they were going down the wrong path with this research. "The purpose is to dispel this craziness."

"Give me this thing." Della Rae confiscated Nicci's laptop and positioned the screen towards her.

Nicci leaned back in her chair, folded her arms and raised her eyes to the ceiling.

Della Rae read aloud as she typed a search phrase, "How to reveal the identity of a ghost," and hit enter. She weeded through the results.

"One way," she read, "is to take multiple pictures of the haunted location. Watch for orbs or ecto it recommends."

"What are those?"

"It says, orbs are circular balls of light and thought to be spheres of spiritual energy. Ecto is an abbreviation for ectoplasm. In regards to spirits, it refers to a gauze-like substance exuded from the orifices of the spirit," Della Rae read.

"Ew," Candi said.

"Exactly." Becca scrunched her nose.

"Oh, here's a link with instructions on how to photograph a

ghost. It says the lower frequency of a digital camera can capture spirits. Most ghosts take on the same appearance as when they were living. It recommends shooting the photo close to mirrors, but not directly into the mirror. It recommends using an ISO of 800 or higher indoors. Who still has a digital camera these days? It recommends a camera rather than a cell phone."

"I do. We can use mine," offered Sherry.

"What do we do once we see the ghost if we even can?"

"Seance, seance." Z chanted, thumping her folded arms on the table.

"Yeah, a seance," Gabby said.

Reading excerpts from another Internet search, Della Rae continued: "Seances are performed to conjure spirits for many purposes. Often the purpose is to contact a dead relative for comfort or for unanswered questions. It says here seances are all about energy. The energy of the group entices the spirits. Holding hands in an unbroken circle maximizes the collective energy. In addition, the people selected for sitting are very important but first, the purpose for holding the seance must be established, clear and understood by all participants."

"Well, easy for us to say. To find out what the ghost wants. Why is she, or possibly he, haunting our studio?"

"What were you reading about the people attending?"

"It says the attendees should value the importance and not think of it as a joke. They should add to the energy. Avoid people who are cynical and will divert the energy."

Everyone leered at Nicci, the skeptic and then at Z, the class clown.

"What? I don't think it's a joke," Z said.

"Well, I'm not serious," Nicci said.

Dell Rae read on. "Also of equal importance is the quality of the medium conducting the event."

"Do we need to find a professional medium?"

"I guess it would need to be conducted at the studio where the ghost's presence is known." Della Rae said. "Although, it does say the location can be a neutral place or a place where there will be artifacts known to the deceased. It also says here, 'Beware, although you may attempt to conjure good spirits, a portal will be opened and dark spirits can also enter and are difficult to get rid of.'"

"Oh, I don't like that," gasped Sherry and waved her hands in the air.

"When should we do this? I know someone who visits a fortune teller. She may know a medium," Della Rae said.

"You find out about a medium, we'll talk to Maggie," Nicci said. "I guess a seance is necessary to disprove this madness."

"I can't take any more ghost talk. Let's shake it off," Sherry said.

∞∞∞

Jewell's gait took on a bounce for her jaunt home. She was buzzing with the energy of the group. She couldn't downturn the grin on her face if she tried. She decided to call Josh instead of text. She filled him in on the ghost talk and the group's plan to identify and rid the studio of the ghost.

"Josh?"

"Yes?"

"I want to tell you something," she swallowed hard. "Remember how we read the same books and discussed them for hours on end?"

"Of course."

"Well, I had other books I read, books meant only for me."

"So, you should have interests of your own."

"Really?"

"Sure, don't you think I find my own interests?"

"Well, yeah, baseball, but I had to keep mine secret."

"Why? Now you're worrying me."

"Because I read about ghosts and witchcraft and extrasensory perception."

"So?"

"Well, we were the smart ones. I'm supposed to be grounded in science."

"You don't think scientists can be interested in the unexplained?"

"I didn't think so. I thought I would seem like a hypocrite."

"Jewell, this goes deeper. You wall up and don't share parts of yourself. What fascinates you is of interest to me."

"There was one other reading interest."

"Yes?"

"I fantasized about being a dancer but knew it was silly. Dancing was for Ashley and Steph from high school. But I still had fun reading about ballerinas and ballroom dancers. It all seemed so glamorous and when I walked into Maggie's studio it resonated with me."

"Babe, that's great. I never realized the connection. Your announcement about starting bellydance classes surprised me and seemed way out of the left field. See, I guess you were supposed to move. By the way, why didn't I ever run across your books? We more or less lived together in college, and lived together officially after college graduation."

"When I moved out of the Thompsons' to go to Washington State, I took the books to the social services department and asked them to distribute them to foster children."

When Jewell ended their call, after sharing her secrets with Josh, she missed him deep in her bones. She resolved to call

Becca the next morning and cancel the concert.

∞∞∞

The next morning Jewell awoke dreaming of Kage and couldn't bring herself to call Becca to cancel. She decided to wait until the next day, Friday, to allow time to pass and build her nerve to cancel.

Her phone alerted her to an incoming text.

Becca: I texted Kage and he is so excited about Saturday.

She carefully considered her reply, not yet prepared to cancel.

Jewell: Me too.

Becca: He wants to know if I can give him your number.

The blood rushed from Jewell's head to her toes leaving her lightheaded.

Jewell: I guess.

Becca: Awesome. BTW, I'm just wearing casual shorts and sandals.

Jewell hated being such a literal person as Becca's text triggered a picture of her in shorts, sandals, and topless at the concert.

Jewell: Okay, I'll do the same.

After texting with Becca, Jewell took Romeo into the back yard. It was sunny, yet breezy. Jewell breathed deep and a blast of renewal and possibility flooded her.

She had a nagging drive to complete her daily check-in with Josh despite the deviation from their normal schedule. If by some chance, she wasn't able to bring herself to cancel the concert, she didn't want to talk to Josh all wrapped up in anticipation for it. She suspected her eagerness would grow as the day progressed.

"Jewell?" Josh answered the phone with an air of surprise in his voice.

"Yeah, my schedule's full with preparations to start work on Monday, so I'm calling early." She hated lying to him.

"Oh, okay. Not much to report here. We only talked last night. Why don't you text when you are ready for bed?"

"What's wrong? Why don't you want to talk?"

"My schedule is full too. It isn't always all about you."

Jewell was taken back by Josh's clipped tone.

"Whoever said it was all about me?"

"Who's in Florida and who's still in Washington?"

"You said I should move."

"I did because you couldn't wait to flee this place and me. But tell me this, why were you hell bent on running clear across the country? Why not Oregon or Nevada? You know, driving distance. Did you ever plan to visit me?"

Jewell heard a female voice in the background. "Who's that?"

"Who's what?"

"The woman there. I heard her?"

"What are you talking about, Jewell?"

"I heard a female voice."

"Oh, the TV. The TV is on."

"It didn't sound like the TV."

"Well, it was. I need to go write. Text me later."

Jewell quickly made up her mind to go to the concert and suffered less guilt over her decision. Maybe it was a good thing she had moved so far away.

∞∞∞

While Jewell sorted through her shorts and tops pondering which to wear, her phone rang with an unknown number displayed. It was a local number so she answered.

"Hello?"

"Jewell?"

"Yes."

"This is Kage. From the diner?"

If Jewell didn't understand anatomy, she would have sworn her heart plopped into her stomach.

"Hi."

"Um, hi. I wanted to check in before the concert tomorrow. Becca said it was okay for her to give me your number."

"Yes, I told her it was okay."

"Good. Now you can save mine. Do you want me to pick you up Saturday? The event is an all-day affair, but we're planning to be there around noon. The food is excellent."

"No, I'll drive and meet you there."

"Text me when you're in the parking lot and I'll come to meet you. I'll find you by searching for the hottest girl in the parking lot."

Before laying her phone down, she decided she should text Josh as he requested.

Jewell: I'm sorry how we left things. I'm not mad. Let me know how your day is going.

Ten

A Concert and Various Other Attractions

J ewell slid into the tan shorts she had bought at the vintage store. They were high-waisted sailor shorts so snug they outlined the booty she was developing from all her walking and bellydancing. She turned left and then right gazing into the full-length mirror pleased with her newly budding shape.

She fussed her hair into a half-up hairdo and secured it with an embellished clip. Her top was a navy and white cropped top. She also spent more time than usual on her makeup and applied the matte red lipstick she and Becca had discovered on one of their shopping trips, Siren Red. The contrast with her blonde hair was stunning.

She rubbed in extra sunblock and threw the bottle into her bag. She had checked the website for the venue and learned she could take Romeo as long as he was on a leash. She speculated he would want to run free, but rationalized he would be happier with her on a leash than at the house by himself.

The two hopped into the Beetle, put the top down, and took off.

Jewell texted Kage: We're here.

Kage: We?

Jewell: For me to know and you to find out...LOL! (She was getting the hang of social texting).

Kage laughed when he caught sight of them and realized Jewell's partner was Romeo.

"See, I told you, you'd find out what I meant by 'we.'" Jewell laughed.

"And I told you, all I needed to do was look for the hottest girl here and I would find you. I was dead on."

Jewell blushed. They walked together to the grassy area where Becca and Renaldo lay on a large blanket. She delighted in Kage's musky scent and soaked in his body heat. She admired his chestnut curls bobbing freely underneath his hat. She had tight ringlets, but his curls dangled loose and soft.

Becca got to her knees as they approached the blanket and called Romeo.

Romeo's whole body wagged as he yanked Jewell toward the blanket. Becca took his leash and romped with him as she introduced Kage to Renaldo. They exchanged pleasantries.

"Are you hungry?" he asked Jewell.

"I am."

They walked to the food truck, ordered fish tacos and took a spot at the end of one of the picnic tables. Various bands were scheduled for the day.

"This band is Quantum Bridges," Kage said. "They play alternative rock. You should hear them unplugged sometime."

"I like them."

"Yeah. The Totally Tubular Band plays next. They play tunes from the eighties. This concert has something for everyone. They hold these to bring the community together."

Jewell pulled Romeo's water dish from her bag and filled it with one of the bottled waters she had packed.

She cleared her throat. "Kage, I promise, I didn't mean to imply there was anything wrong with working on a farm. I don't know of any young people who work on farms or who would be willing to work so hard."

"No problem, I get it. After all, I didn't say, 'Hey, let me go to the concert with that girl who makes fun of me being a farmer now did I?"

Jewell giggled.

"What about you? A scientist. That's pretty amazing. I could say I don't know too many young people who would want to do that."

"You know," he continued, "I think being so family-oriented makes it easier to work on the farm. We are a well-oiled team. Sure we get on each other's nerves sometimes, but what do you have if you don't have a family? What about your family?"

"Becca didn't tell you?"

"No all she told me was I had better go the library and smarten up if I was going to take you out." He grinned.

"Now, I know better. Becca went to a private school and you supposedly went to the same school. I don't know anyone from a private school who needs to be smartened up."

"Touche. I'm stealing your response from the diner, but what about your family?"

"Let's go into my family later. Your band is setting up."

They went back to the blanket. It felt odd being in a semi-reclining position with Kage. The song, "Don't Stop Believin" blasted from the stage. Jewell scanned the festive scene with a mix of people of all ages, some in lawn chairs, and others on blankets, kids ran with colorful streamers, people in the area closest to the band danced and hula hoop dancers dappled the lawn. She marveled over one hula hoop dancer who skillfully handled six hoops whizzing in all directions.

When the band played "Dancing in the Dark" Renaldo jumped up, "Come on, let's all dance."

"But what about Romeo?"

"Bring him."

They danced and laughed. A deep sense of freedom uplifted her, her spirit higher than she ever recalled.

They returned to the blanket and the group of four exchanged small talk, listened to the band and watched the festivities for hours.

"I need to walk Romeo."

"I'll go with you," Kage said.

The sky was pink and blue dotted by a few fluffy clouds as the sun set. They walked Romeo and Kage took her hand with intertwined fingers. It felt like magic.

The sky had darkened when they returned to find the empty blanket. They lay on it together flat on their backs star gazing.

"See the big dipper?" Kage asked.

"Ursa Major."

"What?"

"Yes, I see it." She traced it with her finger.

"Why isn't someone like you taken?" she asked him as he sat up to watch her outline various constellation and clusters.

"Someone like me? What, like a farmer or like a dashing sex symbol?"

"No, young and well, you're right, not hard to look at."

"I had a serious relationship. She took a job in New York. She wanted to stay together, but I couldn't grasp the concept. I don't think the long distance would work for me."

"What's her name?"

"Hope. Oh no you don't, you're not dodging your turn. I'm the one always doling out information."

"Well, I better go, see you later," Jewell joked and sat up.

Kage pulled her back to a lying position on the blanket. He hovered, his upper body above her. Moonlight and festival lights shone providing enough light to gaze into one another's eyes. Her breathing slowed as she melted into a comfortable state.

"Well," he continued. "What about you? Why isn't there a boyfriend? At least I hope there isn't."

"No, same here. I moved to Florida, he stayed in Washington, we didn't want to do the long distance thing either."

"Josh."

"What?"

"His name is Josh. I probably should take Romeo home. I wonder where Renaldo and Becca got to."

"Probably making out somewhere." Kage said, then in a lower voice, "lucky."

"What?"

"I'll walk you to your car," he said. "I was wondering, um, could we go out next Saturday?"

Jewell hesitated at first but then recalled her last conversation with Josh and the female's voice in the background.

"Yes, we could. I mean, I would love to."

"Great, I'll text you with details, unless you have ideas of what you want to do. I just thought since I grew up here, I could come up with a plan."

"No, you decide what to do."

They reached the car. Kage quickly leaned in and kissed her on the cheek, spun on his heels and whizzed off.

Jewell floated home in the Beetle. She sat on her back patio,

Romeo lay at her side, as she sipped sweet tea. The entire day ran through her mind, clip by clip.

Still, no response from Josh. She climbed into bed and texted him again, but drifted to sleep without awaiting his reply.

When Jewell awoke in the morning, she grabbed her phone to check for a text or voice message from Josh. She had slept soundly and thought maybe she missed the notification. But she searched her phone and found none.

He must still be angry. She decided to try again later.

∞∞∞

The drive to work took about twenty minutes. Jewell had made the trip the week prior when her new supervisor scheduled an appointment for a tour of the hospital and lunch with the research department staff. It was a small department where the team worked in close proximity.

Most of the staff had been friendly and outgoing at lunch: however, her supervisor, Gloria, seemed more distant. Jewell attributed it to her supervisory role, until Lacey, the pretty blonde in the same role as Jewell, filled her in. Lacey told her Gloria was an odd one who kept to herself.

Lacey had said, "We all think she's the infamous 'cat lady.' Pamela wore a cat-lady sweater on Halloween and we thought we'd all die laughing. Of course, it went right over the maverick's head, that's what we call her."

Thanks to Jewell's new social life, she had a fresh outlook on life and wanted to make friends at work too. She even decorated her office.

Eleven

A Plan to Perform and A Plan to Photograph

～✣～

Maggie stood before the class to announce details regarding a required performance at the end of this course. She apologized to Jewell stating she had informed the rest of the class before Jewell joined the team.

Maggie went on to explain how the performance was necessary to pass to the advanced class and on to the esteemed induction into the performing troupe.

Jewell's chest tightened with the thought of performing after only eight classes.

"You have terror on your face, Jewell." Maggie gave one of her deep belly laughs then assured her the performance involved the moves already covered and she would allow concessions for Jewell who was at a disadvantage.

"With that said, I'm giving you a treat tonight," Maggie said, as the advanced students slipped through the dressing room door on cue adorned in full costume. They chimed, clanked and sparkled with each step. The superior mystique they carried made Jewell believe they inhabited a universe far above the beginners.

There were six total and if rumors were true, they had been dancing together for years. Some members had flitted in and out, but the core group of six held steady. Jewel had studied their Facebook page and knew their names as Jasmine, Veronica, Emma, Sabrina, Katrina, and Mackenzie.

Maggie said, "They're going to perform for...UGH, DANG IT, THAT DAMN ALARM. I SWEAR."

"We heard about your alarm," the tall brunette, Jewell recognized as Jasmine, said loud enough to surpass the screeching. Her waist-length waves fell as she leaned into the group to continue speaking. Jewell caught a whiff of lavender floating from her hair.

"For us," Jasmine continued, "varying objects drop at precisely 7:10 p.m. every class. It could be a book from Maggie's desk, a—"

She was interrupted by Mackenzie, a much shorter petite redhead. "Oh, and remember when the lamp seemed to propel itself off the table breaking the bulb and we screamed?"

"I almost crapped my pants," Katrina said, the sassy-looking one with short black curls.

"Katrina," snapped Veronica, reprimanding the crassness of her peer. Veronica appeared to be the sensible one with well-groomed strawberry blonde hair, finger and toenails professionally painted the exact blue as her costume and by far the shapeliest troupe member with her ampleness spilling over her costume bra.

"Alright, let's get back to it," Maggie ordered. "As I was saying, the Sacred Moon troupe is going to perform the initiation choreography for you, but don't worry about performing with the same ease they do, they have been at it for a while."

Jewell thought as much as her class encompassed diversity in size, age and life experiences, Sacred Moon personified a more linear arrangement of young, model-looking women.

The beginner class plopped themselves on the floor cushions of purple, pink and gold. The experienced troupe lined up with three dancers facing inward to the right and three facing inward to the left. Jewell marveled at the poise they exhibited simply standing in place waiting for the performance to begin.

The beginner class buzzed with whispers of how great the troupe looked, how they wanted costumes like theirs and how they wanted to hold themselves with such grace.

The Sacred Moon dancers stood patiently awaiting their leader with each outside leg bent at the knee, with the ball of the same barefoot on the floor, heel lifted. Their corresponding hand rested on their hip and their heads were thrown slightly back with easy smiles.

Maggie took her position front and center, clicked on the music with her remote then tucked it in her bra. Unlike the troupe, she wore her typical dance-class attire.

With the first tabla strike, the dancers moved. Confidently, they executed hip drops, basic Egyptians, paddle turns, camels, head slides, snake arms and of course, luscious shimmies. Maggie was right, there were no new moves, but Jewell doubted the moves looked the same on her.

It was a short choreography, over in less than three minutes. Maggie escalated her voice over the chatter of students. The beginner students rushed to the performing troupe to deliver praises for their ability, touching their dangling chains and beads in admiration, asking about their jewelry and makeup.

Maggie pulled a whistle from her desk drawer, blew it, held the thing away from her to exam it and said, "Hmm, I forgot I had this thing." She shrugged. "Okay, break up into pairs of one advanced student with a beginner student, except one of y'all will need to pair with say...Becca and Jewel."

Jasmine paired off with Becca and Jewell, to Jewell's delight. She believed Jasmine was about the closest thing to a movie star she had ever met. Jasmine was patient and kind. This attribute was lost upon a few of the other advanced students.

Becca nudged Jewell to direct her attention to Nicci and Katrina arguing. Emma, the one working with Candi, didn't appear any more gracious. In fact, Jewell noticed Katrina and Emma look at each other often and roll their eyes in tandem.

The time flew and a familiar twinge of dread befell Jewell as the class ended.

∞∞∞

Their walk to Rhita's formed its usual pattern, Candi and Nicci led, Della Rae and Sherry second and Jewell and Becca trailed the procession. Z flitted back and forth between the pairs skipping with the energy of a preschooler.

They got their favorite brews and made their way to their usual round table.

"Tonight was so much fun, y'all," Dell Rae said.

"I'm so ready to perform after watching them," Nicci added. "But I have to say, I got a snotty one who believes she's all that. Doesn't she know how many degrees I possess?"

"I know, and I got the other catty one. Who do they think they are?" Candi asked.

Nicci tapped on her coffee mug with her spoon to gain the group's attention.

"We need to organize our plans to dispel this ghost thing. Even the advanced class thinks a ghost visits them."

"I can bring my camera to class next week," Sherry said.

"A whole week from now?" Nicci asked

"Why don't we ask if Maggie will let us in sooner," Della Rae said. "I'll check with her tonight and start a group text to let y'all know."

That night before going to bed, Jewell texted Josh again.

Jewell: This is getting ridiculous. Let's call a truce. Call or text!

Twelve

A Ghostly Exposure

*T*he next morning Jewell was awakened by a notification from her phone. She had been too wound up to fall asleep until close to three a.m. She hoped it was a response from Josh. Instead, it was a group text from Della Rae. With the passing evenings at Rhita's, the group had all managed to exchange their phone numbers.

Della Rae: I talked to Maggie, y'all, and we can use the studio this evening. She's going to join us and is thrilled we're fixing to get to the bottom of this ghost mess and stop the shenanigans. She suggested we eat at San Sebastian's at seven. I'll make the reservations. Text if you can go so I'll know the headcount.

∞∞∞

The hostess greeted them. "Welcome to San Sebastian's."

Jewell inhaled deep to pull in the fragrance of fresh-baked bread and sizzling olive oil. The scent of sauteing garlic flooded her with memories of Josh. She missed him but extracted pleasure from how her life improved thanks to her move. The move to Florida represented the solution as she had anticipated.

"Did you make reservations?"

"Yes," said Della Rae. "Ten under the name Young."

"Oh yes, Mrs. Young. We're happy to see you again. Follow me."

The group followed one another single-file adorned in clothing they were unaccustomed to seeing on each other. Della Rae led the way in a sleek black dress with a flared ruffle at the right side of the waist, a black fascinator, and basic black pumps. Maggie was behind Della Rae in a silver low-cut, bodycon dress with beads shining in the light and her makeup perfect.

Heads turned to watch the procession with Maggie gracefully sauntering stealing the show. Jewell followed in a pink vintage pencil dress with matching pink heels. She had gone to the hair salon closest to her house and had her hair styled in Victory Rolls. Her matte lipstick in a chalking pink further rooted her 1940s look. Her friends gushed over her transformation.

The remaining procession included Nicci, Sherry, Candi, Z, Miranda, Gabby, and Becca all similarly dressed for fine dining. Even Z had given in to her partner, Miranda's, commands to wear black jeans with a puffy white blouse.

Jewel was too in awe of the high-class restaurant to notice she also turned heads. She soaked in the unique scenery, having never dined in a five-star restaurant. The room cast an outdoor courtyard illusion with amber lighting seeping in from the arched windows. Two stories climbed all four walls holding painted-on windows designed to mimic apartments with balconies as if they awaited lovers to step out and watch the sunset or friends to sip cocktails and enjoy the fresh air. A stone fountain dominated the room. White linen-clothed tables assembled around it.

The waiter arrived in a starched white shirt, black vest and tie. With a quick bow, he presented the menus and offered the wine list to Della Rae, known to the staff from dining there regularly with her husband, Winslow. She was a beautiful woman in her mid-forties, her hair full and shiny with never one black hair out of place. Nothing else would do for a proper Southern lady. Her sophisticated style of dressing and canny talent for accessorizing helped to mask the extra thirty pounds. Her vow to start a new weight-loss diet every Monday amused Jewell.

"So what's the plan for tonight?" Maggie asked.

Nicci took the reins. "We read how images of ghosts can be captured with cameras. A popular belief seems to run through the group," she peered over the rim of her dark glasses to acknowledge each member of the class, "that if we capture an image of the ghost," she used air quotes for the word ghost, "it will supply details about the ghost which may facilitate determining the reason for the haunting."

"The hope is we will be equipped with more information to better hold a successful seance. However, some of us," Nicci pointed back at herself, "believe no image will be captured."

"I'm all for it," Maggie said.

As the conversation continued, the waiter delivered the first course. He laid Jewell's gazpacho before her. It radiated the fresh sent of tomatoes and garlic. She took the terracotta spoon and dove into the cool liquid. The fine texture rolled through her mouth and deposited the perfect balance of oil and fresh herbs. The enjoyment was further enhanced by breaking warm bread and dipping it deep in the seasoned olive oil.

Jewell's food trance broke as the conversation returned to the seance.

"So any luck, Della Rae, with finding a medium?" Maggie asked.

The waiter arrived with the main course and gingerly placed each work of art before them. Joyful exclamations infused the air.

"No, I'm sorry. I haven't had a chance to work on it yet, but I will."

By the time the final course of this five-course meal arrived, Jewell was not sure she could manage another bite. However, her craving for sweets provoked her to order the lightest version on the menu, Natillas de leche. The smoothness of the warm milky substance and the burst of cinnamon mixed with a vanilla scent comforted her like a warm blanket.

∞∞∞

Maggie unlocked the studio door and the group zoomed in.

Striking the light switch, Maggie asked, "Okay how do we do this?"

"It said to take the photo near a mirror, but not directly into it," Nicci said.

"Lights on or off?"

"Let's do both," Sherry said, "and I'll take a ton in rapid fire with the flash on and off."

"You know, she's going to know what we are doing."

"Well, maybe she wants to be exposed. After all, the haunting has increased."

"You know, you all are delusional," Nicci said.

Sherry moved around the room at various angles and levels and snapped photos with and without flash. She waited until all the photos were taken without snooping at the results. She wanted the protection of the group for this task.

When she finished taking photos, her hands trembled. "Want to look?"

The group raked glances from one to another as Z hummed the tick-tock theme from a famous TV game show. They tightened up their formation around Sherry as she held the camera at arm's length so everyone could view.

"Here we go."

The first group of pictures showed flashes of light presumably produced by light bouncing off the mirror.

Nicci said, "See, I told you, a bunch of nonsense."

Then they gasped in unison. There was an outline of a figure.

"Oh no, should we go on?" asked Gabby.

"Of course," snorted Maggie. "Now keep going or give the dang thing to me."

Sherry continued to press the button to move the pictures forward. The next few shots showed increasing clarity of the outline. It appeared to be a woman in a long dress or costume. The final screen in this series revealed the clearest image. It showed a woman in an elaborate headdress with rows of beads dangling. She had rolled curls and a stilted smile. Chunky bangles adorned her wrists. Just as Maggie commented on the bangles, a sound of clanking jewelry rang and they all rocketed out the studio door together, screaming.

Outside, they struggled to catch their breath, even the ever skeptical Nicci.

"Well, we've got to go right back in. This is my studio. I hold my classes here."

"I'm not going in there," cried Z, shaking her head.

"Me neither," clamored multiple voices.

"I will," Jewell said.

"I will too," Nicci said. "I only ran out because you all scared me."

So, the three slowly reentered the studio. Maggie shortly stuck her head out the door and told the rest it was safe. She told them they needed to come right back into the studio so they wouldn't be afraid to come to class.

"Just like riding a horse. Y'all gotta hop right back on the horse. Like rippin' a Band-aid off. Y'all gotta rip it right off. Now get back in here."

The rest of the group reentered looking from side to side and holding on to one another.

"I'll plunge into the seance work," Della Rae promised.

Still staring at the mirror where the image had shown up on the camera, Maggie said, "I think I've seen that woman before."

"What? You know her?" asked Gabby, as everyone turned to Maggie.

"No, I don't know her, she's ancient, but the photos are familiar. I studied dance theology and she resembles a bellydancer I once read about. I think I could find her if we search the Internet. I can't remember the name, though."

"I have my laptop," Nicci said. "Let's go to Rhita's."

Everyone but Gabby left for Rhita's.

∞∞∞

Once everyone had her choice drinks and took their places at the round table, Nicci opened her laptop.

"Look up bellydancers from the early 1900s. Maybe around 1910," Maggie said.

Nicci pecked the keyboard and screeched. With wide eyes, she shifted her view to the group. Everyone piled in behind her to check the screen.

"O-M-G," Becca exclaimed.

"I'm out of here." Z headed for the door only to spin around and return.

"That's her," Maggie said.

"It looks like the image I recall too," Della Rae said and the others nodded in agreement.

"Read it," Maggie said.

91

"This is Wikipedia," Nicci said, as she read:

Clara Tessa Berg, AKA, Alya Raqs[1]

Alya Raqs (circa. 1890-May 20, 1929), pronounced all ya racks, was the stage name of a popular Dutch bellydancer, Clara Tessa Berg, who resided and danced in North America in the early 1900s from approximately 1906-1920. It is estimated she was born in the Netherlands around 1890 to parents Albertus and Helena Berg who later migrated

---

[1] Photo courtesy of Lunagirl Images: https://lunagirl.com/

to the United States with Clara and her older brother Hanns Albertus Berg, estimated sometime in the year 1895. Confirmation of the exact date is not possible due to lost records dating as far back as 1855 from the infamous fire on Ellis Island that burned the immigration station to the ground on June 15, 1897. Clara's father was a talented builder and set up shop in New Jersey. Her father's alcoholism made for a disruptive home life so at the age of 16 years. Clara left her family to take up with a dance company in New York City. She was later kicked out of the group when she was incapable of proving American citizenship. Desperation led her to the discovery of bellydance, an act at the time considered "Hoochie Coochie" and censored. She traveled with a troupe performing in vaudevilles and circuses using the stage name Alya Raqs meaning "Dances from Heaven". She later settled in Southbridge, FL where she perfected her craft and became famous. Her life ended in tragedy at the estimated age of 39 years when her estranged brother, Hanns, brutally murdered her.

"Wow," Jewell said. "They do exist."

"I can't explain the picture, but none of this makes logical sense," Nicci said.

"I promise I will call my friend tonight and we'll set up a seance at the studio," Della Rae said.

"Um, hello," Z said. "Look at her date of death. May 20th. The date is right around the corner."

"Creepy."

"Why, I declare we set up the seance on her birthday," Della Rae said.

"Okay by me," Maggie said.

The group broke up and left Rhita's satisfied with their work.

Thirteen

A Horse, a Buggy, and a Hot Night

I think you should wear the pink floral," Becca said.

"No, the red tight number," Lynn said.

"Oh Mom, you're so out of it."

Jewell couldn't believe she had two women in her bedroom dressing her for a date.

"Which do you like best, honey?" Lynn, Becca's mother, asked Jewell.

"I don't want to hurt anyone's feelings, but I kind of like the salmon colored one Candi picked out when we visited her department store."

"Well, she does know what men like," Becca said and they all laughed.

With her dress, hair, and makeup all perfect, her assistants left.

"Call me," Becca said as she exited the house.

Jewell slipped into her off-white flats and simple silver jewelry.

The butterflies in her stomach fluttered themselves into one big knot. She paced the house; he would be on his way. Romeo followed her in her pacing unsure of the purpose.

The door knocker sounded; her heart knocked louder.

Jewell opened the door to behold her cowboy in dress pants with a suit jacket flung over his shoulder. He had on a tight white shirt emphasizing the muscles farming had built. With no hat, his soft curls fell wildly about. She quickly surmised he had tossed on an extra handful of his titillating musk cologne. She reminded herself to breath and wiggled her toes to prevent fainting.

"Whoa, you look gorgeous, Jewell."

"Thanks," she said, stricken with shyness.

They walked down her sidewalk and through the arbor. On the corner, a white horse and buggy awaited.

"No way," she cried. "These buggies pass me all the time when I'm out walking and I've been dying to ride one."

"Well, die no more. Jewell, this is the driver, David," Kage said.

"And this is Bartholomew," the driver said.

"Hi, sweet boy." She petted Bartholomew's face and neck. "Romeo is going to go crazy when he smells you on me."

"May I assist you into the buggy?" David offered his hand.

"Of course," she said full of anticipation.

It was a bright sunny day, perfect for a buggy ride and a date.

"Aren't you getting in, Kage?" she asked.

"Strike a pose," he said, as he positioned his cell phone poised to snap.

"What?"

"You know, as in *Vogue*."

Playfulness infused her. Whether triggered by the beautiful weather, the charming buggy or Kage mattered little. What did matter was flirtation came over her. The sexy salmon dress didn't hurt either. She mimicked the moves of fashion models in an over-dramatized manner. She leaned forward, touched her chin to her shoulder and batted her eyes; she leaned back, crossed her legs and positioned her hands on her knees, then stood with her hand on her hip and looked away as if she couldn't be bothered.

Kage jumped into the buggy and they laughed. David grinned and asked if they were ready to go.

They rode through the streets and she enjoyed the point of view from on high.

Bartholomew stopped in front of Blue 36 and Vine.

"We're not? No way. Are we eating here?"

"We are if you want to. I made reservations."

"If I want to? Are you kidding? This place looks incredible. Am I dressed okay?"

"You're dressed perfectly," Kage said as he paid and tipped David.

"Ah, the jacket makes sense now," she said.

"No, not necessary, only a collar is required. I wanted to look good for someone." He flashed his sly smile.

"No worries there," she said under her breath.

The opulent ambiance unfolded in the entryway with the high ceilings and chandelier lighting. Deep-brown wood covered the walls and glowed in gold tones from the soft lighting. A harp played in the background. Jewell felt certain it was a recording, but when they entered the dining room, she saw the gold glistening harp and the lovely female player.

Jewell enjoyed the food but enjoyed Kage's company even better.

After dinner, they strolled around the town. The air cooled.

"Are you chilly?" he asked.

"A little."

He laid his jacket over her shoulders and she smiled at him.

"Jewell, we never finished the conversation about your family."

"My story's not as pretty a story as yours."

"But it's your story."

"My father died in a car accident when I was two years old and my mother, well, died soon after." She was developing an unsettling proficiency with the lie about her mother.

"Oh, my." Kage grabbed his chest. "Who raised you?"

"Foster families."

"Was it…was it bad?"

"No, not like the horror stories you hear. Not for me. I would say I was probably ignored more than anything. It was bad for my broth—I mean a friend of mine. Someone from school."

"I'm so sorry," Kage said as he put his arm around her.

"One more turn of a corner and we'll be back at your house. Do you want to do anything else first?"

"No, I'm good," she said, the mood a little darkened by talking about her past.

They reached the door. Romeo ran to Kage. After a bit of attention, she told Romeo to go in.

She stood with the door open and Kage in the doorway.

"Want to come in?"

"Nah." He peeled loose paint from the door jam. "Well, I guess I ought to go?" He kicked a few loose pebbles from the sidewalk into the grass. "Do you want to go out again?"

"I do," Jewell said, conjuring a breathy voice. Then she couldn't help herself, "Are you applying for a painter or gardener position?"

"What? Oh yeah, you're funny. Someone should quiet you."

"Are you going to peck me on the cheek again and run away?"

He moved closer, placed his hands around her waist, leaned down to her lips and kissed her soft and slow. It was a wet kiss, wetter than any other. Electricity zapped her lips, not the kind from static, but deep exhilarating electricity ignited a fire inside her. Their breathing hastened. She threw her arms around his neck and thrust her body against his. When she considered curling her leg around his, Romeo whined.

"It's okay, Romeo, go lay down."

The devil and the angel fought again. Ask him to come in again, the devil coached her. It's too soon, you know what will happen, the angel argued. The angel won this time and Jewell slowed and eventually halted the kiss. They both sighed. They stood close and he fidgeted with her necklace.

"I'll go this time. I'll be in touch about our next date."

"Perfect." She gave a big sigh and leaned in the doorway to watch him descend the sidewalk and climb into his truck.

∞∞∞

Jewell sat on her bed basking in the afterglow. She checked the antique clock, five minutes after midnight. She stretched out on top of the covers and rubbed Romeo's head. She heard her phone.

Becca's picture displayed at the top of the screen with a text.

Becca: Hey, where are you? I'm not interrupting, am I?

Jewell: Nah, I'm home.

Becca: Alone? LOL.

Jewell: Of course. Um...Hello...first date. Remember?

Becca: I'm in town. Bottle of wine in the car.

Jewell: Okay, come on.

The pair sat cross-legged on the floor, an arrangement Becca initiated so she could wrestle with Romeo.

"So, how did it go? And don't leave out one detail, not one."

Jewell took a sip of her wine after she had swirled it around in one of her favorite wine glasses to admire the deep red hue.

"He stood at my door with those gorgeous light brown eyes locked with mine; his lips were curled in a smile. Only, he wasn't a cowboy tonight."

"Aw, darn."

"No, no complaints here. He had on dress pants and a jacket flung over his shoulder. His musky cologne was stronger than usual."

"I love his musky scent," Becca said and they both sighed.

"He told me I looked gorgeous and—"

"And you did. Sorry, go on."

"He couldn't seem to take his eyes off of me. Even when others addressed him, he held his gaze with mine."

"Oh, and did I tell you about the horse-drawn buggy?"

"You're kidding."

"And a real harpist played at the restaurant?"

"Shut the back door."

"He sent pics to my phone of the evening while we strolled through town."

They scooted together to view Jewell's phone.

"Look at you posing. You go girl."

They slapped hands in a high-five.

"You ate at Blue 36 and Vine?"

"We did."

"Okay, so now the juicy stuff."

"He kissed me."

"How was it?"

"It was magical, and I'm telling no more."

"Oh, you." Becca threw a sofa pillow at her.

"I'll tell you this, I was close to tempting him in, but I don't want to blow my chances."

"Jewell, I don't think you could blow anything with Kage. I watch how he looks at you."

In her state of happiness, Jewell truly hoped Josh had found someone too. She hoped the female voice she heard in the background was a new love interest. Maybe he wasn't texting out of guilt. She would clear things up and put their friendship back on track.

"Hi, this is Josh. Leave a message and I'll get back to you."

Fourteen

A Dark and Never-Ending Flight

❧⟳❧

As content as Jewell went to bed, she awoke the opposite. She still hadn't received a response from Josh.

She went to the kitchen, made her coffee, and checked her phone.

She had a message from Kage.

Kage: Last night was a blast. I can't wait to do it again!

She smiled.

She scrolled to Josh's chain of text messages. No response since Friday. No return call. She was worried. She decided it had been long enough and would insist on a response.

"Hi, this is Josh. Leave a message and I'll get back to you."

"I've been texting you and I called. I know we didn't leave things so good the last time we talked, but we said we would be friends for life if nothing else. I don't care if you're seeing someone. Please call me back. I'm getting worried."

She wished they had more contacts in Port Eastlyn so she could call someone to check on him, but they had kept at arm's length from others. She determined her brother Nathanael would be no help. Besides, she and Josh had their secrets to keep and it was best if they handled them.

A text notification sounded and she swiped the screen with urgency. It was Becca.

Becca: My shift at Rhita's doesn't start until five p.m. Want to go to lunch?

Jewell: I don't know. I may end up having to fly back to Washington.

Becca: What?? Why, what's wrong?

Jewell hesitated, and then ticked the keys on her phone.

Jewell: I have a family emergency.

Becca: I thought you didn't have a family.

Think, think, she told herself.

Jewell: Well, someone like family.

Josh consisted of her true family.

Becca: Can I help? Want me to come over?

Jewell: Nah, thanks though.

Becca: What about Romeo? I can stay with him.

Jewell was not used to such generosity. She had planned on taking Romeo but admitted to herself he would be happier staying home.

Jewell: Maybe? If you can? That's a lot to ask.

Becca: You didn't ask. Besides, are you kidding me? A night away from Lynn and Brook's arguments. What time is your flight?

Jewell: The flight isn't booked yet.

Becca: Do you think you'll book it for today?

Jewell: Yes, if I can swing it. Oh gosh, that reminds me, I'll need to call my supervisor.

Becca: I'll find someone to cover my shift at Rhita's today.

Jewell: No, Romeo is fine here for a little while by himself.

Once I know the flight time, I'll get the house key to you.

Becca: Okay, keep me posted.

Jewell made travel arrangements which included an hour drive to the airport in Crystal City for a flight taking off at noon. So much for being thrifty, she thought, with the cost of her flight nearly $1,000.

Becca arrived at Jewell's house not waiting to hear back which relieved Jewell who rushed through the house in preparation for the trip.

"I got Brittany to cover my shift. Does Kage know you're going?"

"Oh, no. I didn't even think about it."

"No worries, I'll tell him. If you want?"

"Sure that would be great. I appreciate you staying with Romeo. Here's his food. I feed him two cups in the morning and one in the evening. I keep his water bowl full at all times."

"My return flight is scheduled for one p.m. tomorrow and then I'll have the hour drive back. I didn't even ask, do you work tomorrow? I know you don't keep a set schedule."

"I'm off tomorrow so I'll be here when you get back."

They hugged and Becca wished her luck in whatever her undertaking.

∞∞∞∞∞

The window view Jewell had so strategically scored fell short of its promise. Instead, it offered a jet-black sky, a black so dark it reminded her of the color of her biological mother's hair, although it was a vague memory. The black canvas lay splattered with gray clouds from a paintbrush devoid of pigment.

She strived to draw in the pleasant aroma of fresh-brewed coffee wafting from the back of the plane, a fragrance far sweeter than the mix of body odor and some spicy cover-up cologne

104

from the rotund man next to her. He wore a comb-over in some apparent attempt at an optical illusion. It didn't work. His cologne competed only with a stench she identified as stale cigarette-smoked clothes, Channel No. 5 and Aqua Net emanating from the blonde with a beehive. She occupied the aisle seat. Aqua Net? Jewell wondered if they still made that stuff.

The lit seatbelt sign trumped the serving of coffee. "Aqua Net" fidgeted with the pink silk scarf she retrieved from her neck and "Comb-over" who spilled into Jewell's seat, snored in rhythm with the rain pummeling the metal craft.

Thunder cracked and the plane dropped forgetting to take Jewell's stomach with it and then leveled only to drop again.

The lady from the aisle seat turned to Jewell in a clear attempt to engage in conversation. Jewell pondered over the breach of flying etiquette. Anyone who flies knows you don't talk to the person next to you, of course, unless doom lurks.

"I'm Jean. Are you coming or going?" she asked her voice gruff, Jewell suspected, from decades of smoking.

That's a great question, Jewell thought as shrill cries from an inconsolable baby blasted from a few rows back. The engine surged and roared.

Jewell raised her voice to speak over the noise. "I guess I'm going? I mean, I lived my entire life in Washington, in Port Eastlyn, but recently moved to Florida. I'm Jewell."

The plane jostled again, but neither conversation nor turbulence could awaken the large man between them who let out an ear-drum busting snore. Jean and Jewell looked at him then to each other and shared a chuckle at his earnest commitment to sleep despite the turbulence, thunder, and crying babies.

"How about you?" Jewell realized her weeks in Florida were changing her. Prior to her move, this conversation with a stranger would have been shut down, and fast.

"I live in Seattle. I was visiting my grandkids in Dallas. They are the light of my life. I lost my husband a couple of years ago."

"I'm sorry."

"It's okay now, but I sure miss him. There is nothing like a happy marriage. How about you? Are you married? Any kids? Although, you're awfully young."

"I'm not as young as I look. No, no husband or kids yet."

"Boyfriend?"

"Nope."

"Well as beautiful as you are, it's only a matter of time. Are you coming to Washington to see your family?"

"Sort of."

"What type of work do you do?"

Jewell launched into her spiel about work and answered the inevitable question about how someone her age was so accomplished.

The plane descended without incident despite the weather and earlier turbulence. Jewell and Jean exited the plane together. Jewell hugged her newfound friend, something unfathomable prior to the Florida move, and then made her way to the car rental counter.

∞∞∞

The eight-and-a-half-hour flight landed her in Seattle at 11:30 p.m., Pacific Time. The prospect of the unbearable drive from Seattle to Port Eastlyn increased her angst. The only rental left was a humongous boat of a car, a Lincoln Town car, something she imagined a grandfather of hers would drive if she had a grandfather.

She paused prior to leaving the parking lot to text again. No response. She called and immediately heard the voicemail greeting. No sense in leaving an umpteenth message.

The windshield wipers flapped and scraped in spots with a squeak trying to keep up with the dumping rain as she gripped the steering wheel and leaned forward in some attempt to propel the car forward faster.

A slight chill ran through her as she pulled into the driveway of the pink Victorian she had left behind.

"Damn." She realized she had left her key to the apartment in Florida. No problem, she appeased herself. She fantasized Josh would answer the door, tell her his phone had crashed and he had changed carriers but was so busy, he forgot to tell her he had a new number. They would laugh and catch up with each other. Besides, if he, by some weird fluke had gone out, she knew where the spare key was hidden.

A crazy thought crossed her mind as she recalled the unknown female voice she had heard in the background of their last phone call. If Josh had liked staying at Jewell's apartment so much when they were in college, maybe he liked staying at the mystery female's home?

"DAMN," she shouted louder this time. The flower pot on the porch rail no longer housed the emergency key. She searched other potential spots unable to comprehend any reason for changing the hiding place. After all, they had established the spot the first day they moved in and it never changed.

The pungent odor seeping from under the door made her think he mustn't have taken the trash out for days.

The darkened downstairs apartment and missing RV told her Frank and Marcia were on one of their trips. The other upstairs apartment still appeared vacant. She banged on the door. No answer.

Left with no other foreseeable option, Jewell gave in and

called Rocky's certain to reach Nathanael. Her big brother was predictable if nothing else. She needed to call the bar since her brother refused to own a cell phone. He attributed his aversion to cell phones as a way to avoid evil technology, but Jewell suspected it was more likely related to dodging authorities and debt collectors.

The bartender passed him the cordless phone. "Hi, little Sis. How's Florida? Sunny? Get it?"

"Yeah, you're a riot. I'm here. In Port Eastlyn."

"What the hell? Why?"

"Josh isn't answering my calls or texts and now he isn't answering the apartment door."

"Calm down spaz. I'll be right over. Chubo is probably cowered in the bathroom or something from the storm."

She paced the porch picking at her cuticles until they bled. It seemed an eternity until Nathanael arrived and skillfully slipped his credit card in the door jam opening the door with a creak.

"Holy shit, what the hell stinks like gut-rot?" Nathanael crooked his right elbow to cover his nose with his arm.

Jewell took a deep breath, held it in and grabbed her brother's other leather-jacketed arm as they entered the dark living room. Being familiar with every nook of the apartment, she flipped on the lights, an act she wished she could take back.

"Ah, oh my god. JOSH!"

"Son of a bitch, Jewell," Nathanael exclaimed.

She rushed to kneel beside him on the living room rug. Her anatomy and physiology studies clued her he had been dead for days. Despite the disgust of his body's decaying appearance and smell, she laid her head on his furry sweater, a dress style he carried through the years. She whispered through tears, "Josh, I'm so sorry."

"Shit, he's dead. What do you think happened? Do you think he finally lost it and did himself in?"

"Ahhhhh!" she howled. "I think I did it."

"What the..." he bounded away from Jewell and the body.

"No, the drugs." She spewed rapidly, with no filter, "We had a new promising drug almost finished phase three and I couldn't wait any longer. He refused to go to doctors anymore. He was spiraling downward worse than ever so I took a chance and snuck them home. He was doing better than ever. He was going out, even by himself. It was a miracle. I didn't think I was taking a risk, other than the risk of getting caught. I swear, I carefully reviewed the data. No one had any life-threatening side effects."

"Oh hell, oh hell..." Nathanael continued to pace. He pushed back his thick black hair, exposing the creases in his forehead, his classic handsome face rugged with stubble.

"Okay, think, think," he said.

Jewell remained knelt at Josh's side.

"Okay, we need to get rid of the body," Nathanael said, throwing his hands from his hair to his sides.

"What? No. No way. Are you out of your mind? We need to call the coroner."

"And say what?" he mimicked her voice, "Um, I brought him medicine illegally and had him take it without a doc's say so or monitoring and um, now he's DEAD. Wise up, you got all the book smarts. I got the street smarts. No one is going to give us any breaks. There's no choice unless you want to spend the rest of your life in jail, no, hold on, I'm not going down with you so we have to take care of this."

She pulled out her cell phone and he ripped it from her hand.

"Nathanael, I mean it. I am going to handle this properly. I'm going to call 9-1-1."

"What are they going to do, bring him back to life?"

"No, but the cause of death is unknown."

"But we know the cause." He continued to hold her phone too high for her to steal back.

"I'm not going to tell them I suspect the cause. Do you think I'm stupid?"

"Then let's bury him."

"NO!" Jewell screamed. "I will not. First of all, it would make everything ten times worse when his body is discovered, and they always are. Second of all, he is someone I loved, love. Third of all, following the proper channels is the right thing to do."

"So now you're worried about the right thing to do?"

"Nathanael, I told you, none of the participants in the experimental arm had any major incidents."

"Speak English."

"Of the ones actually taking the drug, they experienced nothing but minor side effects. I'm not leaving, Nathanael, until I call the police."

He hurled her phone at her as he darted for the door. "You're making a big mistake. I don't want any part of this. If they find out you were giving him drugs, man, and it killed him. At least give me a head start before you call."

"Nine-one-one, what's your emergency?"

"Yes, I found my boyfriend on the floor. I'm sure he's dead. Oh god. I don't think he needs EMS. He needs the police or the coroner."

The drugs, she thought. They might search the apartment. She went to the dresser drawer where they had stored them. She gasped. No drugs, no containers. Beads of sweat amassed her forehead and the back of her neck.

She flung boxers and socks from the drawer. Nothing. She

stuffed the contents back in the drawer to avoid suspicion then flew to the kitchen where she slung and banged drawers. Nothing.

She scoured the apartment. Her breathing transformed into pants. Beads of sweat morphed into streams trickling down her face and dripping to her shirt. The bathroom. No drugs, no containers.

Her whole body shook. Oh, no, did he take too much? By accident? On purpose? But she found no signs of overdose. Did she miss something?

She went back to where his body lay. No pills or bottles around him, no signs of anything he used to wash them down, and no overt signs of aspiration.

It appeared he had plopped to the floor suddenly causing her to believe, to her horror; it was the accumulative effect of daily ingestion and no further monitoring after she moved. She had monitored him for months and he was doing well with normal vital signs and no side effects. Guilt pierced her like a dagger as she jolted from a knock on the door. It was the police and coroner.

They stood side by side. The burly police officer stood about six foot two, weighing about 230 lbs. and in contrast, the coroner, a small man about five foot nine, 145 lbs. The officer was in uniform and the coroner in jeans and a navy jacket with a state logo.

"Jewell Caldwell?" the officer asked.

"Yes."

"I'm Officer Blevins," he said, his puffy, round face expressionless.

"You made the nine-one-one call?"

"Yes, sir."

He peered through the door, his gaze tight on Josh's body. "Are you the victim's next of kin?"

Victim, she thought. "I am his only family. We are not blood relatives, but we are each other's powers of attorney. Well, I guess, I'm just his now."

"What's the victim's full name?"

"Joshua Frederick Anderson."

"Hi, ma'am, I'm Dr. Abraham. It's nice to meet you." The smaller man held out his right hand.

"You too." Jewell accepted his hand.

Officer Blevins shot him a frown.

"When did you find the victim?" the officer continued.

"Excuse me one minute," Dr. Abraham said. "Did he see a primary care physician? Was he examined in the last thirty days?"

"Goodness no," Jewell said. "I wish he would have had a regular doctor."

"Under the circumstances, an exam will be necessary since the cause of death is unknown."

"The time? When did you find the victim?" Officer Blevins repeated.

"Oh, I guess it was around one a.m. or a little later?"

"Your call was placed at 1:28 a.m. Do you live here with the victim?"

"No, I moved to Florida on March 9th."

"Of what year?"

"This year," she pulled back to look at him, her brow furrowed.

"Did you live with the victim prior to your move?"

"I did. We stayed in touch daily after I moved, but he stopped responding to my texts and calls."

"When was that?"

"It was... Let me look at my messages to be sure." Jewell pulled her phone from her pocket and scrolled through the message chain. March 25th. That's right, she forgot, it was the night before the concert. "It was March 25th. I continued to text and call him and then, I flew here."

Dr. Abraham had been examining Josh's body. He called to Officer Blevins, "I would estimate death occurred in the same ballpark of time, about a week or so ago. We won't know for sure until the autopsy. Thank heavens for the cool Washington springs."

"What time did you find the body?"

"Right before I called you."

"Do you still have a key?" He inspected the door.

"I do," she lied, and folded her arms to hide her trembling hands.

"And why didn't anyone else in this building report the stench?"

"The neighbors below are out on one of their camping trips and the apartment next door has been empty for a long time. It's not in as good of shape as this one. Plus as you can see, the house is far from other homes or buildings."

"I see," he said. "I need to look around. Make sure there are no signs of foul play. Someone may have broken in and no one would have heard."

"I, I understand," Jewell said.

Officer Blevins headed for the kitchen.

Jewell stared at the open bedroom door, her whole body quivering. She remained in the living room with her arms wrapped tightly around her belly.

"Do you need to sit ma'am?" Dr. Abraham asked.

She concentrated on trying to relax her appearance. "No, I'm fine."

She tracked the officer as he inspected every room of the apartment.

He finally concluded his search and returned to where she stood. "Nothing seems out of order. I need your contact information, Ms. Caldwell." He flipped to a new page in his notebook.

"I'll go retrieve the gurney, ma'am." Dr. Abraham left the apartment.

"I have all I need. I'll be in touch if I have any more questions," the officer said, and then he left.

Dr. Abraham returned with the gurney and a young assistant. They placed Josh in a body bag and then lifted him to the lowered gurney and then returned it to it's higher state. Dr. Abraham zipped the bag.

"Wait," Jewell cried. "Can I say goodbye?"

He shot a sideways glance at his assistant. "You can, but I have to ask you not to touch the body."

She kept her gaze on Dr. Abraham as she walked towards Josh's body with trepidation.

She whispered as close to his ear as she could stretch, "We had such good times in the beginning, didn't we? I'll never forget my chubby redhead in the front row. Remember our movies and our walk home when we both got our first kiss? Then the passion in the Thompsons' upstairs, our fun early days in college. And then," she paused. "Forget the bad times, I will. You were my childhood friend. I loved you from the first day in ninth grade and I will love you until the day I die."

She sniffed and wiped her eyes with her sleeve. "Okay, you can take him." She stepped back toward the door.

Dr. Abraham zipped the bag past Josh's face and pushed the gurney toward the door. He paused when he reached Jewell and leaned in, "I'll stay in touch, ma'am. Reports are normally completed in seventy-two hours, but we're really backed up.

We're in the throe of an opioid epidemic, you know. Young bodies show up left and right and we have to perform the exams. Damn shame." He shook his head and clucked his tongue.

"Officer Blevins will put your information in the system and I'll call you once I know anything." He handed her a business card and touched her shoulder.

"Do you know which funeral home you would like us to contact?"

"Oh, I didn't even think about that. Weinbrener's Funeral Home, I guess. The one on Woodland Avenue."

"Yes ma'am, I know where Weinbrener's is located."

"He talked about cremation." Funny, she thought, how he caged himself up in the apartment but didn't want to be trapped in a coffin.

"Is there anyone who can stay with you?"

"What? Oh," she shook her head to throw off the trance, "I'm heading back to Florida."

When she was alone in the apartment once again, she combed every room in anguish, foraging for the remaining drugs and still found nothing. Convinced the drugs couldn't be in the apartment, she had no choice but to give up.

She gathered Josh's most prized possessions, the books and articles he had written and his photos of Jewell and of his grandmother. She searched the desk drawer and halted at the manuscript, *The Mansion Marked for Murder*. She ran her hand over it, anxious to read it on the plane. She had room in her carry-on to stuff the manuscript and some articles, but the rest she would arrange to collect later. She would need to return to Port Eastlyn to collect his ashes.

115

Fifteen

A Flight Home through Josh's World

A s she read the words, "The End", she laid the manuscript on her lap and gave a tiny clap. She marveled at his ability to make a murder mystery touching. The deep point of view of the detective and the lively descriptions plopped Jewell in the middle of the story and pulled her into Josh's world for the flight home.

When she arrived at her Florida house she startled Becca and Romeo with a thump of the front door. It banged into her hallway tree with Romeo's leashes, the rain jacket she could have used on her trip, and walking shoes.

"Oh, I'm sorry," she said in a soft voice, but not soft enough, as Romeo sprang to his feet and bounded at her with enough force to knock her off balance. It dawned on her they had never spent a night apart. She squatted beside him and he soaked her with sloppy kisses.

Becca threw her arms above her head for a stretch and yawned.

"We were taking a nap. We fell asleep watching TV. "How was your trip? Is the emergency resolved?"

"Oh, it was okay. A false alarm," Jewell bit her lip to hold back the tears.

"See, I told you it would be fine. Everything always is."

Jewell wished she could believe Becca and wished, even more, she could be so optimistic. But, Jewell was practical and everything did not look fine from her perspective.

"Did you sleep at all on your trip?"

"No, I didn't."

"I guess not with such a grueling itinerary. Why don't you try to sleep now?"

"In the middle of the day?"

"Sure, why not?"

"Well, let's have some wine first then," Jewell said.

"But it's only two o'clock in the afternoon."

"Yeah, but I'm willing to bet I can find a beach sign somewhere in this house..." she looked around, "...reading, *It's Five O'clock Somewhere.*"

"Ya got me there. Bring it on, sister."

They sat on the back patio and tossed Romeo his ball this time.

"Do you want to talk about your trip?"

"Not really, if you don't mind."

"What on earth happened to your nails?"

"I got bored on the plane and picked at them." She curled her fingers into a fist to hide them.

From there, the conversation consisted of small talk including more funny stories from Becca's past. Jewell found this a relief, not being up to conversation herself.

"Did Kage call you?"

"He texted. Nothing much. He was checking how my trip was going and how we would make arrangements for our next date when I returned."

"Awesomesauce," Becca said with a wide smile.

"Your eyes are heavy. Do you think you can sleep now?"

Sleep, Jewell wondered. How could she ever put Josh out of her mind long enough to relax and sleep? Yet, the wine, the long trip and more of Becca's stories made her think it possible.

"Maybe I should try to sleep some."

"When are you going back to work?"

"The day after tomorrow."

"Text me when you're up."

Becca hugged Jewell and left with her backpack over her shoulder.

∞∞∞

Sleep came to Jewell from pure emotional and physical exhaustion yet in the middle of slumber she bolted to a sitting position startled by an alarming nightmare about Josh.

They were floating in a rowboat, she couldn't think why since they had never been in a rowboat together. Regardless, they floated at night and fell asleep side by side in the vessel, but she awoke to his stiff cold body, his eyes wide with fixed pupils.

She screamed and sprang up in the boat, provoking enough turbulence to throw him overboard into the deep waters. She labored to catch him but failed. She sat in bed breathing rapidly, her arms clutched to her chest. Romeo placed his front paw over her and pushed her back onto the bed.

Disoriented, she noted the time read five p.m. It was still Monday. She had slept most of the day. Good, she thought for she predicted the passing of time would be her friend now, each new day relieving the pain bit by bit. She didn't delude herself with hopes of the pain ever completely leaving her but counted on the extreme ache in her throat and belly to ease enough to at least eat again.

She also thought of the guilt. Had she caused his death? She couldn't bear to dwell on such thoughts. No, she had to stay active. More answers would come with Dr. Abraham's report.

∞∞∞

Jewell arrived at the studio to find Nicci, Della Rae, and Z standing at the top of the stairs. They nudged her view toward the studio door where Maggie stood twisting her key, taking it in and out in an apparent attempt to unlock the door.

Maggie looked back at her students. "She's trying to keep us out now, I guess so she can have the place to herself. First, she tries to scare us off, now this, but I'm not giving in. Do you hear me?" She pounded on the door.

Becca, Candi, and Sherry joined the group.

"What's up?" Becca asked.

"Oh, we're watching to determine the winner, Maggie or the ghost."

"I'm going to win." She fiddled with the lock. "Hey, why don't y'all talk about the costumes you want for the performance. You've made it this far, now it's time to invest in some costumes."

Candi started with a bellydance call Maggie had taught them, "yip, yip, yip," and the rest joined in.

"Where can we go?"

"There aren't any shops around here," Maggie said. "You can buy online, but that isn't as much fun and finding the right fit is almost impossible. Plus, don't think I haven't noticed y'all like to pal around. So I suggest going to Crystal City to Desert Rose's. She gives our troupe a ten percent discount."

Gabby arrived late and commented on the excitement of the group as they continued to stand outside the studio.

"Wait, what did I miss? Y'all are usually inside ready to go when I rush in, I mean arrive." Gabby laughed.

Della Rae filled her in on the jammed lock and the shopping trip.

"I want to go too," Sherry said.

"We're all going," Della Rae said. "How about this Saturday?"

"I can't go," Candi said. "I work every Saturday."

"Well, let's look at another day."

"No, like no problem," Candi said. "I mean, I'll be working the next few Saturdays since we are running promotions, or whatever. You should all come by. Support a girl, ya know?"

"I won't be able to go either," Gabby said.

Maggie finally gave up on getting in a conventional way and forced open a ground-level window, slid her slim body through it, landed on the floor and unlocked the door from the inside.

The class flooded in, buzzing about the shopping excursion. Della Rae volunteered to drive stating she had enough room for all six.

"So let's land on a date then," Nicci said.

"I vote we keep it this Saturday," Becca said.

"Me too. Sorry Candi and Gabby," Z said.

"It's okay, we can order online," Gabby said.

"Okay, then, this Saturday it is and I'll drive," Della Rae said.

Jewell mulled over a reason to excuse herself from the trip. She was still grieving and worried about the autopsy results, but she couldn't let it show.

"Do we need a particular costume style or color?" Nicci asked.

"You should buy Egyptian style, but, then again, that's all Desert Rose's carries. You can choose whatever color you want," Maggie said.

"Y'all need to come up with a troupe name too. I've decided you're going to be your own troupe and I'm making an intermediate class for y'all to move into next."

Class proceeded as usual with more work on the choreography in preparation of the performance. Jewell was getting the hang of the routine and beginning to think she would be okay with performing.

∞∞∞

On the walk to Rhita's, Nicci stomped in the lead with Candi at her side. Her arms flailed in an apparent rant.

"Alert ahead at twelve o'clock." Della Rae slowed her pace and awaited Becca and Jewell, nodding toward Nicci. "She's pitching some kind of hissy fit."

Nicci and Candi halted causing the others to stop when they reached them. The group formed a circle on the sidewalk.

"You all realize what's going on, don't you?"

"What, pray tell, are your panties in a wad about, Nicci?" Della Rae asked.

"Yeah, what?" Z asked.

"Don't you get it? The Snobby Moon troupe doesn't want us in the troupe or class with them."

"Sacred Moon," Becca corrected.

"Call them what you want, I call them Snobby Moon," Nicci said.

"Oh, I get it, funny. See she's playing on the words..." Z faded noting no one else was smiling.

"In addition, Maggie doesn't think we are worthy of moving into the advanced class."

"I think you're overreacting," Della Rae said. "Let's keep going."

They arrived at Rhita's and their round table was taken. They pulled two tables together in front of the window.

"Wherever shall we meet for the shopping trip?" Della Rae asked.

"Um, I might have to work. I missed a couple of days this week and need to catch up," Jewell said.

"Oh no, man, were you sick?" Z asked.

Becca and Jewell exchanged glances.

"No, I had to go out of town."

"Please go, Jewell," Becca said. "Can't you work extra on Sunday?"

"I don't know, I guess."

"Yay." Becca clapped her hands.

"Let's meet at the Park and Go on the other side of the bridge," Nicci said. "I Googled Desert Rose's and it opens at ten a.m. so if we leave around 8:45 a.m., that should be about right."

"When did you Google it? Whatever, okay, 8:45 a.m. Saturday morning at the Park and Go. So that's five of us, right? No wait, I forgot to count myself," Della Rae said.

"Yep." Becca pointed around the table, counting aloud and landed on six.

"Still, I think we should talk about being overthrown by the advanced troupe."

"I don't know, Nicci, do we really want to be in a troupe with others who don't want us?" Becca asked.

"I agree, besides, we are unique," Z said.

The women reached consensus to build their own strong troupe.

Sixteen

A Shopping Trip where a Troupe is Born

T he morning of the shopping trip, Jewell awoke dreading it. Faking happiness turned out to be tougher than going without it. Work proved a safer haven these days where she could drown herself in work and where faking happiness wasn't a requirement.

Neither could she bring herself to set another date with Kage. His persistence burdened her further.

Jewell managed to muster enough courage Saturday and met the others at the Park and Go. She pulled into the lot next to Becca's car. Becca waved and opened her car door.

"Hey, Becca."

"Hey, Jewell."

"Where's Della Rae's Lexus?" Jewell searched the lot for her very distinctive car, a four-door Lexus with custom Metallic-Satin-Cashmere paint. Jewell had asked her about the paint color, being familiar with ordering a custom color."

"She's over there in the new Suburban. Everyone but Z is in it already. I was waiting for you."

Z arrived and climbed into the car with the rest.

"Whoa, nice ride," Z said. "Is it new?"

"Thanks. It is new. And there's a story behind it."

"It must be a good story," Becca said.

"Oh it is, but a long one. We'll get into it later."

"Should we talk about names for our new troupe?" Becca asked.

"How fun," Sherry said, "picking a name for our troupe."

"I'm glad you brought it up, although I was planning to address it. I made a list," Nicci said.

"Of course you did," Della Rae said under her breath, but loud enough for the others to hear.

"Well, I just made a list of possible words to include in the name, that's all. The group can put the words together to form a full name. I'm not a control freak."

"Fair enough," Sherry said. "What do you have?'

"Yeah, fire away," Z said.

Nicci passed each a copy of the list of words she had gathered. "Dancers, gypsies, warriors, sisters, daughters, treasures, hips, wings, cloak, veil, mystical, sky, lotus, Southbridge, rising, crimson, wild, secret, Kashmir, silk, rose, goddesses, desert, rain, and oasis. I can come up with more if we need more."

"Ew, I like something with Kashmir," Becca said. "How about Daughters of the Kashmir Rose? Wait, I guess a rose wouldn't be Kashmir."

"Or, Gypsy Warriors," Z said.

"Why, I rather like daughters something. It makes me feel younger," Della Rae said.

"I'd like to have a wild secret," Sherry said, sparking a laugh from the group. "But in all seriousness, how about Desert Goddesses or Mystical Desert Goddesses?"

Jewell sat gazing out the window.

"Jewell, hello, we asked what you think. What name do you like?"

She refocused and reviewed the list.

"The name of Maggie's studio is The Sacred Veil Studio, but the other troupe has sacred in their name. Maggie's stage name is Maggie of the Silk Veil, so what about, Sisters of the Silk Veil?" Jewell asked.

"Brilliant," Z said.

"Yeah, Brilliant."

"Agreed," Della Rae said.

"You named the best one yet," Sherry said.

"Nicci?" they asked.

"I have to admit, it is a pretty logical name." Nicci smiled at Jewell making it a first.

∞∞∞

The suburban reached the shop parking lot. Desert Rose was the size of a warehouse. They entered in awe of the wall-to-wall costumes and jeweled accessories arranged by color. The decadence yanked Jewell from her funk and she was catapulted back to her youthful days and dreams of dancing.

"I've been trying to decide if we should all chose different colors," Nicci said.

"Well, Sacred Moon has different colors."

"I guess they should complement one another though?"

"Okay, let's choose colors before we branch out," Nicci commanded.

"I have dibs on red," Jewell said.

"Yes, Jewell needs red to go with Siren-Red lipstick," Becca said with a wink.

"I want dark purple," Nicci said.

"That will look way cool on you," Z confirmed.

125

"I want gold um, harem pants. Sorry, I'm not feeling the dress thing," Z said.

"Perfect, Z," Becca said.

Sherry chose royal blue and Becca, silver.

"I'll take teal. I'm told I look finer than frog hair split four ways in teal with my black hair and all." Della Rae fanned herself with her hand and blinked rapidly.

"Sherry and Gabby will have to choose different colors."

They spread out in search of their respective colors. Becca and Jewell went together first to Becca's silver section with rows and rows of silver costumes of various tones and shine.

"Do you want shiny silver or more of a gray?"

"Yeah more of a gray, maybe, with silver accents?"

They narrowed the search down to Becca's size and plowed through the hangers.

"Hey, when is your next date with Kage? Are you going to fill me in?" Becca sifted through the abundance of costumes.

"No, no date set yet."

"What? Why?"

"We haven't coordinated a convenient time yet."

"When did you get so busy? You couldn't wait for the next date."

"I started working, remember? I need to be sharp. I'm in new territory in a hospital. I'm facing a learning curve, you know."

Becca raised her eyebrows. "Alrighty, I hope your schedules, and other things, mesh soon." She nudged Jewell with her elbow.

Jewell pulled out the glitziest item she had ever seen, a silver bra and belt set so gleaming in the overhead fluorescent lights, she had to squint. The belt dipped into a triangular point in the front and back. Ample rows of fringe swung from the bottom. The bra/bedla plunged in the front holding the same abundant fringe.

"I love it," Becca said as Jewell offered it up. "It needs a skirt, but I'm not thrilled with the grays, what about a white satin one?"

"Yes, good idea. No one took the color white yet. So I say you get two colors."

They scurried to the white section of costumes where they scored the perfect skirt with slits on both sides.

"Ooh-la-la," responded Jewell, warming up further to the shopping trip.

"Let's find my costume and then look at the bling."

"Deal."

Finding the sea of red was easy. Becca held her new skirt draped over her arm and the hangers with bra and belt in the same hand as she flicked through the red selections with her free one.

"Oh, Jewell." Becca pulled a bra and belt set from the rack, gold, and red endowed with oval turquoise beads and a bright silk skirt with slits similar to hers.

Jewell loved it. She thought of the girl in the foster homes hiding dancing books and never once believing she was worthy of such a beautiful costume.

They rushed to the dressing area together to find Z already in her gold harem pants with surprising openings from ankle to hip, a gold belt and shiny gold top of which she told them the sales lady called a cholis.

The dressing room area consisted of several separate dressing rooms within a sizable curtained-off section housing full-length mirrors on both walls so the shoppers could step out to the common area for a full view or to solicit feedback.

Becca and Jewell entered the same dressing room giggling like school girls. Jewell emerged and studied her image in the mirrors as Della Rae and Nicci pulled back the curtains to enter.

Della Rae gasped at Jewell's image.

"Between you, Candi and Becca, no one is ever going to take a gander at the rest of us on stage," Della Rae said.

"I disagree," said Nicci. "The audience will be looking for the best dancer."

"Not the men. What dream world do you live in?" Della Rae asked.

"You're slaying that red costume," Becca said to her best friend as she stepped out of the dressing room into the common area.

"Look who's talking," Della Rae said to Becca. "You both look like you belong on the cover of Bellydance World, if such a magazine existed."

After everyone had purchased their costumes, they went to lunch then rode to the Park and Go. Becca and Jewell stood at their cars parked side by side.

"Do you think you'll end up scheduling a date with Kage for tonight?"

"No, that would be short notice."

"Want me to come over later?"

"Don't you have a date with Renaldo?"

"No, he's going out with his guy friends."

"Sure, if you want."

"Ok, I'll let you know."

Neither pursued it further.

∞∞∞

The next week at class, Maggie informed the group they were making great progress and would be ready for the performance in June. She encouraged them to begin stirring interest in their families and friends to attend.

Walking up the steps of Rhita's, Jewell noticed a crowd at the place across the street, something she had never noticed before.

Inside Rhita's, they found their regular round table available. Nicci bustled over and set her executive bag on one of the seats to reserve the table.

Renaldo was working and Jewell observed as Becca skillfully picked up her school-girlish smile and waved.

The group converged on their round table with drinks in hand and discussed the upcoming performance and seance.

"So, I have an idea," announced Z.

"Oh no," Sherry said.

"No, hear me out. So, I think our troupe is unique. We don't fit in any mold. So, my thought is what if we surprise Maggie and come up with our own little choreography to tack on the end of our performance?"

A lengthy pause ensued.

"But we don't know how to write choreography," Sherry said.

"No, wait a minute," Della Rae said, holding her hand in a stopping gesture. "I think this might be fun."

"What on earth would we do?" Nicci asked.

"I found some fun music. I don't know if Maggie would care for it because the style is a little more fusion, but whatever. I study videos and I like the more contemporary stuff."

"Maggie doesn't like contemporary," Becca said.

"Yeah, but she has a good sense of humor," Z said.

"Selective good humor," Sherry added.

"It's worth a try," Della Rae said. "I have a big house. I'll text some dates and times along with my address and we'll match up what we can pull together."

Jewell worried about having another choreographed dance to learn.

"Not to change the subject, but did you secure a medium yet, Della Rae?" Nicci asked.

"I did, I spoke with her on Monday. She is able to schedule one on May 20th at Maggie's at 8:30 p.m.," Della Rae told them.

"May 20th is a Friday. Why so late in the day?" Nicci asked.

"She said she needs it to be dark. There are candles involved. What's your problem? You better not come if you're going to be all negative."

"Oh, I'm coming alright. I'm ready to quit talking about this nonsense."

"The time is fine with me," Becca said. "I think we can all sacrifice part of a Friday evening. How long did she think it would last? There should be time to go out afterward, right?"

"She said it depends," Della Rae said. "And another thing, Nicci, why did you even start taking classes in the first place? You don't strike me as someone dying to join a group for social or any other reasons, oh, unless, of course, it promotes your career."

The others passed wide-eyed glances from one to another.

"Well, if you must know, and apparently you must, my husband got it in his head I needed some female friends," Nicci said. "He bet me I couldn't join a group and stick with it. I proved him wrong."

"Sorry Becca, back to your question." Della Rae shook her head. "She said it depends on whether she is able to connect with a spirit or spirits. She said this town is a hotbed of spirits and people have seances all the time to reach a certain spirit and conjure up all types of others. So the times vary."

"Cool," Jewell said.

"Yikes, I don't like that at all." Sherry grimaced. "That's too creepy."

The music from across the street grew louder. The bass reverberated through the coffee shop.

"Who's up for dancing?"

"Awesomeness! A dance party." Candi sprang from her chair causing it to tip backward and strike the floor.

"I'm up for it," Sherry said.

"Me too." Becca leaned towards Jewell whispering, "I'm going to go behind the counter and check if Renaldo can come. Why don't you text Kage and ask him to meet us?"

"Come on let's all go. No excuses," Della Rae said.

Seventeen

A Place across the Street and to Top it Off, An Alley

❦

*T*he tavern across the street, named The Wooden Gimlet, in keeping with the era it was built, had groups gathered on the front lawn all the while a line snaked through the front door. The air was muggier than usual causing a haze.

Jewell blinked hard to clear her vision thinking she spotted Nathanael leaning against the tavern in a curious way. He had his arms crossed in front of him with his right leg bent and his foot flat on the wall gazing toward Rhita's, clearly not part of any group.

Her blink didn't clear the image so she smiled and waved. Her stomach knotted a little thinking of the circumstances of their last encounter. Then the male figure eerily resembling her brother walked away without waving back, so Jewell realized she was mistaken.

Once inside, they made their way to the bar through a sea of people. Candi led the way as she squeezed through the crowd to the counter never missing a chance to flip a suggestive smile at the cutest guys.

She called back to the group "What do y'all want to drink?"

Becca, the group barista, committed the requests to memory and assisted Candi.

It was a small tavern bursting with more people than Jewell guessed the fire code would allow. The log cabin style building possessed the same rustic aura as Rhita's, only instead of squeaky floors, this one had sticky beer-spilled floors.

"Quantum Bridges", the letters on the drum set spelled. The band she had heard at the concert with Kage. Kage, she thought. Had he responded to her text invitation?

As she reached for her phone, she saw him enter. He wore his tight jeans, T-shirt, cowboy hat, and boots causing her heart to flip in her chest. She had to remind herself the plan was to cool things off. He fought to make his way to Jewell through the crowd.

Maggie, who to Jewell's delight met up with them, wasted no time hitting the dance floor and joining some of her advanced students. Maggie's beginner students surrounded her, dancing to her lead astutely adding the bellydance isolations to band music.

Della Rae and Maggie, the happily married ones, appeared content with dancing. Sherry lagged at the bar too engrossed with her tequila to dance and Z was busy dirty dancing with Miranda.

Miranda was a sweet girl with a beautiful face, a smile as kind as Z's, and burgundy-streaked hair. Her round body contrasted with Z's athletic one.

Nicci said only moments after arrival she had to leave for some work project. Candi ran off to a dark corner with one of the hotties she had spotted on her way through the crowd. Jewell and Becca danced with Maggie until Kage reached them.

"Want a drink?" Kage asked.

"No thanks, I still have one somewhere." She scanned the room. "Oh yeah, at the bar near Sherry."

"Come on, let's go. I need one. How about you Becca?"

"Yeah, I'll come with you until Renaldo gets off. I'll search for an open spot to sit."

The crowd forced Jewell to walk close to Kage. She felt his heat and inhaled his musky scent nearly melting her into a giddy teenager. Her strong attraction to him flooded back, blotting her memory of why she had been avoiding him.

They retrieved their drinks and spotted Becca leaning against a wall.

"No seats open, sorry," Becca told them.

"No problem. We can stand," Kage said.

"Hey, did you see Sherry?" Becca asked.

"Yeah, I tried talking to her earlier to drag her out on the dance floor and she couldn't string three words together," Jewell answered.

"I'll keep an eye on her and once Renaldo gets here, we'll make sure she makes it home."

"Aw, good idea," Jewell agreed.

The man Jewell had mistaken for Nathanael entered the tavern. The distance to the door was not enough to mask the certainty this time. It was him. He beckoned her to come to him.

"I have to go." Jewell handed her glass to Becca.

"No. Why?" Kage pleaded.

"I agree. No. Why?" Becca said, through tight lips and glaring eyes.

"Romeo's been in too long. I need to let him out."

"I can go with you," Kage said.

"No, I have a work thing to take care of too," she replied.

She couldn't stay for any more responses. She headed for the door and Nathanael standing next to it. As she approached him, he opened the door and nodded his head to direct her outside.

"Come on, follow me."

∞∞∞

Nathanael led her to the narrow alley behind the tavern. "What are you doing here? I knew I saw you earlier. I waved, but you didn't see me," she said.

"Shut up," he commanded, his stern tone unfamiliar as he grabbed her wrist and pressed her back against the brick building.

"We've got a problem. I need money and you're carrying a secret what could land you doing big time so you need to pay up or your secret gets busted."

"What are you talking about?" Jewell's brain grappled to discern between reality and nightmare.

Maybe he was joking around? But the feel of his tight grip as he clenched her wrist and the dampness penetrating the back of her shirt pressed against the building told her otherwise.

"My version is, you stole this drug from your job and gave it to him to do him in. Then you disposed of the drugs and confessed to me so I could help you rid the body, but I talked you out of it and made you call 9-1-1. I struggled with keeping this secret and had no choice, but to turn you in."

"You know that's not true."

"Just you and me there. No one else," he reminded her. "I'm sure if they dig around, they'll find drugs missing from your big research place."

She had thought about injecting a virus into the database to crash the system. Her hacking covered her trail, but bringing the system down would have erased it clean. But she couldn't bring herself to ruin the system.

135

"How much money are you talking about?" Each word pierced her throat like a shard of glass.

"Nough to get out of this jam and live like you. You're the one got all the breaks, hotshot."

Through a squeaky voice, she said, "I can try to pull together around fifty thousand in a couple of days. Meet me under the edge of the bridge on this side, Friday at ten a.m. Then will you go back?"

His warm breath struck her face, spewing a stench of cigarettes and cheap whiskey.

"What, and leave my little sis and her cute friends?" he taunted loosening his grip. "I know what he got in that settlement. All of Port Eastlyn does. It'll do for now."

Jewell stood alone stunned and chilled despite the muggy Florida air. A salty tear reached her lips as she longed to go back in time, back to the hopeful drive along the coastal highway, filled with anticipation for a happier life.

She couldn't believe she had missed this side of Nathanael. They didn't have the opportunity to bond like brothers and sisters brought up together, but they lived in the same small town. She thought she knew him.

Memories flooded her like a tsunami as she toiled to make sense of this turned-up world. She recalled a conversation on one of his birthdays, right, his sixteenth birthday. She remembered because she could only find a "Sweet Sixteen" card in pinks at George's County Drug, a small-town drug store later turned into one of those big chains with an acronym for a name.

They had met at the old-fashioned family restaurant with jukeboxes at every booth. He seemed angry that year, resentful, restless. He had gone on about how she got better foster homes because of her brains and quietness and he got stuck with the "pisshead" alcoholics and child abusers.

"Are you alright?" she had asked the day of his sixteenth birthday celebration. "Let's go to the social services department and change your family or maybe move you to my foster family, no, wait, they can't take another, but let's move you somewhere nice," she had said.

He had gone into a rant to educate her, she assumed, on the real world and how some are born for breaks and others aren't. He called her a blonde princess.

It hurt like a gut-punch. She hadn't witnessed such anger in him again, until the alley.

Jewell walked home alone in a daze as she contemplated a plan to provide Nathanael with the money. She would have to move funds around to withdraw such a large sum. He wouldn't be able to deposit cash in that amount without raising suspicion. On the other hand, she was hesitant to write a check which could quickly be traced back if he did end up reporting her role in providing the pills to Josh. She would have to come up with another way.

Her concentration was broken as the hairs on her arms rose, piloerection her scientific brain told her, the bristling of hairs due to involuntary contraction of small muscles at the base of hair follicles from a reflexive response of the sympathetic nervous system to cold, shock, or fright. Hers was a reaction to the certainty of someone following her, but she turned around and couldn't find anyone. The eerie sensation followed her home.

∞∞∞

Thick fog hovered over Southbridge like a veil. Jewell drove the brand-new black Mercedes titled to Nathaniel Caldwell to the Stallion Bridge.

He had dropped his given middle name, Miles, after their mother abandoned them. While they were still in their mother's care, something he had more memory of than Jewell, their mother had explained to him the name Miles came from their mother's father.

However, Nathanael dropped the name out of resentment toward the maternal grandfather who neither he nor Jewell had ever met. The story went, Miles had abandoned his family, teaching his daughter it was acceptable to cut and run when things became too stressful.

Nathanael was waiting for her as planned and she handed him two key fobs and a clear title. What he did with the vehicle afterward was none of her concern. She preferred this method of delivering the funds to him. She rationalized the trace might be less likely to pop up.

She also handed him a cell phone she had purchased.

"What's this? You know I don't use those damn things."

"We may need to stay in touch over this and how else will I contact you? Besides, I bought it and will pay the monthly bill. No one will have your number but me."

Nathanael accepted the phone.

She picked up on something subdued in her brother. The transaction was completed and they parted ways. She wondered if she would ever lay eyes on him again and it caused her to wave as he drove away.

Eighteen

A Best Friend Stolen

~ ∂♡∂ ~

*T*he next Wednesday after class, the round table held other patrons again. The women ordered their drinks and pulled the same tables together in front of the window. The group was pretty much segmented into pairs due to the table arrangement and the noise from the coffee shop. It was crowded.

A tear in the corner of Becca's eye caught Jewell's attention.

"Oh no, what's wrong?"

"Renaldo said he doesn't want anything serious. He said he had planned to date other girls all along. He said he loves my company, blah, blah, blah, but he can't be with only one. He said he would love me to be one of the girls he dates."

"Oh no."

"Exactly, I can't do that."

"I'm so sorry."

"I'm alright." Becca wiggled in her chair to sit up straight and replaced the tear with a smile. "I met someone else already."

"Wow, that was fast."

"Yep, he started coming to Rhita's and flirting with me. He's dreamy."

Becca and Jewell left Rhita's together. Jewell's heart sank as she experienced deja vu, spotting Nathanael across the street at the tavern. He was leaning against the building in the exact same stance as last week, the night he had pulled her into the alley.

She narrowed her eyes at him and frowned wondering what he had in store for her, but he relaxed out of stance the same time Becca moved away from Jewell's side.

She couldn't believe her eyes as Becca rushed to Nathanael and they embraced. Becca slapped on the same school-girl grin she wore with Renaldo. She turned back to Jewell and waved goodbye.

Jewell took off for home stomping her way through the streets of Southbridge nasals flared and fists clenched. The night was hotter than usual even for Florida. If anyone was watching they would peg her mad, as she yelled, "How dare him. That son of a bitch. Poor Becca has no idea who he is, but he knows who she is and what he's doing. He's doing this to get to me. He knows I'll be forced to protect her."

The hairs on the back of her neck and arms rose again along with the same eerie sense of being followed.

She reached home with record speed, driven by a thousand forms of rage, her neck drenched in sweat. She slammed the door behind her, propelling objects to fall from their positions with thuds and bangs. Some flew across the room.

She regretted this action and the hostile energy it emitted into the room. It was an energy and noise so intense it caused Romeo to startle and yelp. He had never experienced Jewell this way and he required a good bit of TLC to be consoled.

Jewell thought, all her life she had taken whatever she was

dished. "Not this time, no, not this time," she proclaimed.

Refocusing on Romeo, she took a deep cleansing breath shook her arms and legs to purge the tension like runners do before a race. She walked Romeo outside to soothe him.

Outside he wagged his tail and the spring returned to his step. She stopped and knelt next to him kissing his curly face. She dropped Romeo at home and set out on foot.

She leaned against Nathanael's apartment building arms crossed and right leg bent placing her foot flat on the wall gazing toward the road awaiting his arrival.

He appeared spooked when he glimpsed her mocking the identical stance he had used to taunt her.

"What? How the hell?" he reacted to her unexpected presence.

"How what? How did I know where you live? How did I know when you would be home? I have my connections," she said in a cool voice she hardly recognized.

She let the explanation lie there, not tipping him off she added a tracking app to his phone and linked their two phones prior to giving it to him. It was an app designed for families to keep each other safe, only she was using this one to keep herself safe from him. He would never be aware of it, thanks to the feature allowing parents to hide the app from their kids.

"Now you're going to listen to me this time." She assumed she caught him off guard because something stunned him into silence. Maybe it was the fact she had located his apartment or perhaps her sudden brazenness.

"You are going to leave Becca alone. I don't care what else you do. I wish you would go back to Washington, but if you leave me and my friends alone, do whatever you want. You think you hold something over me? Well, guess what? I think you're bluffing. The last thing you need is to draw attention to yourself with the authorities. I have a clean record. Can you say the same? I'm a scientist contributing to society. What have you accomplished? Do you think they're going to believe you over me? I'll tell them I found you at the apartment searching for money and I have no idea what must have happened that night. The whole town knows what a bully you were to Josh."

She shocked herself with the nerve she had somehow acquired but assumed unique courage must result from the constant bombardment of one tragedy after another.

This time, Nathanael was the one left standing stunned and speechless.

∞∞∞

Jewell went home and sat on the back patio with Romeo. She thought about Josh's death and Nathanael's blackmailing. They robbed her of her desire to socialize and have a life. She thought maybe she was sentenced to the life of a loner, only now she would truly be alone because she didn't have Josh.

She concluded the fortitude to continue with bellydance and the trips to Rhita's had left her. She could no longer pursue the happy path she had started on all the while carrying such misery and guilt. Still, she would need to at least keep in touch with Becca to protect her from Nathanael.

It was late, but she knew Nathanael was home so Becca would be too.

"Jewell is everything okay? You called me, did you mean to text?"

"No, I meant to call. I didn't wake you, did I?"

"No, I'm on the same pink cloud mom accused me of before."

"Oh, it must have gone well?"

"It did," she sighed. "Did you get a good look at him?"

Jewell took advantage of being on the phone instead of in

person and rolled her eyes before she replied, "I couldn't make out much of him from the distance."

To Jewell's misfortune, Becca launched into a litany of vivid physical descriptions.

"He's so muscular and his hair is so dark and thick and wavy. He's got wide sideburns and the perfect amount of facial stubble to make him sexy. It tickled my face when he picked me up to draw me to him as he kissed me goodnight. I could measure his strength and oh, did I tell you he has these worry lines on his forehead making him look mature and tragic? He's like a rugged mountain man gone bad-boy. I could have floated home after his kiss."

The last thing Jewell needed was an account of her brother's physical attributes. Girls and women had been losing their minds over him as far back as she could recall. But Becca didn't know what festered inside.

"Jewell? Did you hear a word I said?"

"Oh sorry, Romeo was chasing something. Um, yes, he looked attractive from across the street. Are you meeting him again?"

"Are you outside this late?"

"We are. We're on the back patio. Now you were saying about the next date?"

"Before we kissed goodnight, he said he wanted to see me Friday. We're supposed to meet at the tavern again at eight p.m."

"Original."

"Uh?"

"I mean, that sounds great." Jewell drummed up the cheeriest voice possible. "When will I hear about the date?"

"I know, let's go to the mall the next day, Saturday morning, and I'll tell you all about my delicious night. But don't make it too early, I might be out late." She giggled. "How about eleven?"

"Sounds good, I'll pick you up at eleven Saturday morning. Wait, what's your address?"

"I'll text it so you can save it in your phone."

∞∞∞

Saturday morning, Jewell drove to Becca's as instructed through the gate and around the circular drive to the massive brick home where she lived with her family.

The brick staircase led to the porch and narrowed at the top spanning wider and wider toward the bottom until it reached the drive. Manicured shrubs and flowers lined the front of the house.

She arrived at the oversized front door and pressed the button, rendering the slow deep reverberating sounds, "Ring, ding, dong."

Becca flew out the door and grabbed Jewell's arm. "I'll show you around next time. Mom's delivering a lecture to Brook and believe you me, you don't want any part of it."

They climbed into the Beetle.

"How did your date go last night?" Jewell held her breath for the answer as she pulled out of the driveway.

"He didn't show. I was going to call you but felt like such a fool so I came home and cried to Mom."

"Oh no, I'm sorry." Jewell was sorry for Becca. Sorry she ever got messed up with Nathanael, but at the same time, both relieved and amazed he had heeded her warning.

The mall was small compared to the ones in Seattle, but it possessed the typical bright lights and in-your-face commercialism. Jewell much preferred her downtown shops. They strolled through the stores and Jewell touched an item or two with little interest.

"What do you want to look for?" Becca asked.

"Nothing."

"Nothing? Then why did we come here?"

"Because you wanted to."

"I was trying to think of something we could do together."

"This is fine."

They walked through a few more stores. Jewell found it difficult to conjure excitement for Becca's tie-tops or the charms she riffled through to add to her already weighted charm bracelet.

Jewell couldn't help thinking Becca had no idea what it would feel like to be in her shoes, Becca, with her perfect childhood and perfect life.

"Where do you want to eat lunch?" Becca asked, in what sounded like a forced hearty tone.

"It doesn't matter," Jewell answered.

"Aren't you hungry? How about dessert instead?"

"No, I'm really not hungry."

"Then let's just go."

"Why?"

"You don't want to shop. You don't want to eat. Let's go."

Becca went through the mall door and didn't wait to hold it for Jewell. She stormed ahead of Jewell toward the car.

"Slow down," Jewell yelled.

"Why?"

"So I can catch up."

Becca stopped and turned to her. "Why do you care if I slow down? What's wrong with you? You don't text with me like we used to, you don't want to do anything together, and you've got Kage going out of his mind."

"What do you know about Kage?"

"He tells me about it. He can't talk to you. You won't make any plans with him."

"Stay out of it."

"Oh, don't worry, I will."

Jewell pulled into the Steals' driveway and Lynn leaned out the front door to beckon Jewell in.

"The coast is clear, Brook is in her room," Lynn called to Jewell, laughing.

"That's okay, Lynn, maybe the next time."

"Bye Becca," Jewell said as Becca climbed out of the Beetle and went inside without looking back.

∞∞∞

Jewell found some comfort in knowing Nathanael had stood Becca up, but she still needed to keep an eye on him. She checked her tracker and noted something very odd. His GPS showed him in Washington, in Port Eastlyn.

How could this be? She had been checking the tracker at least daily. He was in Southbridge yesterday morning. She didn't have the heart to check her tracker while she thought he was on the date with Becca.

She set out on foot for his apartment.

The block was fairly vacant where his apartment building sat. It was on the outer perimeter of town, on a street where traffic was allowed. The building is a square brick building and on quick assessment, she guessed it could hold eight equal-sized apartments, four in the front and four in the back. There was no sign of the Mercedes.

She found a couple cozily entwined on the stone steps at the apartment entrance. His arms were around her waist and hers around his shoulders.

"Excuse me," Jewell said, "do you know the dark-haired guy who lives in one of these apartments?"

"Oh, the mysterious guy? The real hottie?"

Her partner protested, "W-T-F. I'm right here."

146

"No matter," she went on, "yes, he lived in this bottom one. His apartment's empty now. Want to rent it?"

"He moved out?"

"Yeah, I watched him climb into a cab yesterday. He didn't come with much and didn't leave with much. Real mysterious. I called before he closed the cab door and asked if he was going on a trip and he said a permanent one."

"What about his car?" Jewell asked. "I thought he used to have a Mercedes."

"You know him?"

"A little."

"I don't know. That car sure was out of place here. It was almost as hot as him."

The girl's partner protested again.

"I know he had a for-sale-sign stuck in the car window," she told Jewell.

"Thank you."

∞∞∞

Jewell carried her new resignation to being solitary into the next week. Monday afternoon at work branded her a loner even further when she sat by herself at lunch.

"Where's your cute cowboy on this rainy day? I thought he was going to make a habit of picking you up for lunch when it rained. We didn't want to miss him," Lacey said, stopping at Jewell's table before passing.

Kage had taken her to lunch twice on rainy days by copping an excuse with his dad about the rain hindering his work on the farm. He told her his dad realized they had enough inside work to keep him busy for several days, but he let him go anyway.

"Uh, I don't know," Jewell said, not sure how else to answer.

"Aw, I'm sorry. Guys are such jerks," Lacey said. "Want to go to

147

for drinks after work?"

Jewell didn't want her pity. "Thanks, I'm sorry, but I already have plans."

"Well, let me know if you change your mind or want to talk."

"Okay, I will."

Nineteen

A Mystery of a Female Solved

J ewell sat in her living room in front of her computer, the way she used to in the bedroom of the Washington apartment. It was a habit she hoped she had banished forever.

She had been far too busy to waste time in front of a computer after her move to Southbridge with her new her new friends and adventures filling her hours, but here she was again. The only problem was there were no dream towns to explore. She had found the best location and there was nowhere else to place her dreams.

She had stopped going to class. Della Rae and Z texted. She had no real answers for her absence to offer.

Her phone rang.

"Jewell Caldwell? Is this you, ma'am?"

"It is."

"Ms. Caldwell, this is Dr. Abraham. Do you remember me?"

"Of course."

"I need you to first confirm Joshua's full name, date of birth and the last four digits of his social security number. Forgive me, these are part of the standard operating procedures."

Jewell satisfied him with her responses.

"The autopsy has been completed and the body is released to your custody. I can contact Weinbrener Funeral Home, but you'll need to call them about the arrangements. I think you mentioned cremation? You can discuss the details with them. I will email a release form. Please sign it and send it back to me as soon as possible and thanks for getting the POA paperwork to Officer Blevins."

"I'll take care of the release form, but what about the autopsy results?" her heart sank.

"I'm able to provide a summary of results over the phone and then you may request to have a formal report mailed to you. The funeral home will have the death certificate."

"Yes, please. I would like to know." She took a deep breath and braced herself.

"You know his congenital heart defect—"

"What? No, I had no idea he had any heart issues. He resisted visiting doctors. He had a lot of fears."

"Well, he was born with this defect. It predisposed him to heart failure and cardiomyopathy, a fancy word for an enlarged weak heart."

"Yes, I'm a scientist," Jewell imparted to avoid minute descriptions.

"It was the cardiomyopathy that killed him. His heart wore out. He appears to have died suddenly and most likely didn't suffer."

"Ugh," she gasped and slumped into her chair. "I'm so grateful to hear he didn't suffer." Her lips quivered. "What a relief. How about anything in his system?" She dared ask, but purposely avoided the term "drugs." She held her breath awaiting the answer.

"No, there was nothing in his system. No chemicals detected. He mustn't have been on any medications. Shame he wasn't under medical care for his heart."

"Yes, a shame for sure. Thank you, I will make arrangements with the funeral home."

"I'm sorry for your loss. Oh, and I have a note from his pocket. It has a woman's name and phone number. Do you know Mindy Sigel?"

"Mindy Sigel, no, I don't. What does the note say?"

"Just has her name and phone number. Do you want the number?"

"Uh, yes please." She recorded the numbers he recited.

"Again, sorry for your loss."

Jewell fell to her knees in front of Romeo and hugged him tightly. She sobbed for Josh, for his sweetness, for his friendship, for the mental torment he endured, and for his love of her.

If only he had told her about his cardiac issues, but it occurred to her he may not have known. She thought of how aloof his mother had been and, like Jewell, he had little family to speak of other than his grandmother. She did her best, but she was limited due to her age and her own health issues. It was possible his heart condition had never been diagnosed.

She remained on the floor with Romeo as Dr. Abraham's words sank in. He said Josh had nothing in his system. How could this be? Why didn't the medication show up? She could recite the chemical compounds and they would have shown in the analysis. The realization deepened. He couldn't have been taking the drugs. The drugs didn't kill Josh. *She* didn't kill Josh. The snowballing tension of these last weeks vanished from her body causing her muscles to go flaccid.

∞∞∞

"Hello, is this Mindy Sigel?"

"It is," a peppy voice answered.

"My name is Jewell Caldwell."

"Oh Ms. Jewell, I heard about Mr. Josh. I'm so sorry."

Stunned, Jewell asked, "Do I know you?"

"No, but I feel like I know you. Mr. Josh hired me in February. I'm in my senior year at John Ricker High. I posted an ad in the paper he worked for looking for after-school work as a personal assistant, you know. My grandfather gave me the idea. He said with the biotech company being the largest employer in Port Eastlyn, surely with the long hours the employees work, they could use help around the house or running errands. I have a lot of energy and Pop said it would be good for me."

"Oh," the girl laughed, "what a surprise finding me must be. He didn't want you to know about me or worry about him needing help or he says you would have hurried right back here and given up on your dreams and how he didn't want that..."

The chatty girl finally took a breath and Jewell used the opportunity to interject, "And Josh hired you? I had no idea."

"I know, like I was saying, he told me he didn't want you to know. He hid how bad he was feeling. And…" She stopped.

"And, what?"

"Um, you know his medicine? He didn't want to worry you or anything, but he didn't want to take it anymore because he said any of the medicine he took made him foggy and he couldn't write and how he would rather stay in the apartment and be able to write than to be on the medicine. He told me it was top secret. He said you wouldn't like it and his doctor wouldn't like it."

"I don't understand. He was getting better."

"Ms. Jewell," she said in a calmer tone, "he hired me to help him

152

and run errands so he wouldn't have to go out. I think I kept him entertained." Her speech perked up again. "I would distract him by telling him silly stories about my little siblings and he would laugh. I told him about my drill team events and the boy I liked. He wasn't much on words, but I can talk, no problem you see. I don't find it hard at all to find things to say. They come to me like magic or something. It's a gift. I really like him. Sorry, liked him."

"Me too."

"He said he figured for some time you were going to leave," Mindy went on seldom coming up for air, "and how he wanted you to have everything you ever dreamed of and everything you deserved and how he couldn't stand in your way so he fought to convince you he would be alright with every intention of going off the medicine once you were gone. He told me how you made sure his doctor gave him plenty of pills because you knew he wouldn't refill them often once you were gone. The plan was after you left, he would rely on me to bring him food and supplies. He knew he could go back to concentrating on writing if he didn't have to spend such energy pretending to be better. He loved to write and it made him happy."

"Um, you said he stopped taking his medicine. Did he have any of his prescription left?" Jewell bit her nails.

"Well, he got rid of them. He said since he wasn't taking them anymore, it wasn't safe to have them lying around. Anyway, he had me buy kitty litter one day and I said, Mr. Josh, you don't have a cat. He told me that was the safest way to dispose of unused drugs. Who knew? So I bought it for him and the next day I came back and he had it ready for me to take out in the trash."

Jewell sagged against the wall for support.

"Now I feel awful," Mindy babbled on. "I shouldn't have gone away. I should have stayed in town. I had taken off for a beach trip for spring break. Mr. Josh said he would only need me every two weeks. I needed to supply him enough groceries to get through a few weeks and he had my cell number in case he needed anything suddenly and I could get someone else to pitch in. He also had deliveries set up."

"So I texted him when I got back and he never responded, which was unusual. So I went to the apartment the next day. I had my own key, you know. He gave me the spare one from the flower pot. I opened the door and the apartment was empty. I looked all around for him, but couldn't find him and I knew that was odd with him not going out or anything. I had the landlord's number and she told me he died and you had the apartment cleaned out and the lease stopped. Oh gosh, is this my fault for leaving?"

"No, it sounds like you did everything you could for him. The coroner said it was probably sudden and he likely didn't suffer. I plan to call the funeral home today to make arrangements. Josh used to talk about cremation so I'm sure that is what he would want. I'll call you once I've made arrangements."

"Thank you, Ms. Jewell."

Twenty

A Dark Night Breaks into Light

J ewell's relief of being certain the drugs didn't kill Josh and of how he took care of her by disposing of the medication and telling Mindy he had a doctor was overshadowed by her return to the solitary activity of web-surfing.

A knock at the door sounded. Romeo barked and jumped to his feet. Jewell was startled. She squinted through the peephole. It was Kage.

She bit her lip contemplating her next move.

"Jewell, I know you're home. Your car is parked out front. So you're not driving and when you're out walking, you have Romeo and I hear him. So..."

She opened the door slowly.

"Hi," she said.

"Hi."

Her gaze was drawn to an envelope in his hand, about the size of a greeting card.

"How have you been?" he asked

"Okay."

"Where have you been?"

"Here and work."

"Yeah, I heard you quit going to bellydance and Rhita's. Becca said she hasn't talked to you in a while."

"You and Becca sure worry a lot about who I'm talking to and who I'm not or where I'm going or where I'm not."

"We call the worry caring about someone, Jewell." His voice rose another decibel, enough to nab Romeo's attention.

"The last few weeks have been rough and I need to be alone. Having friends and fun doesn't seem to work out for me."

"Having friends means you share your rough times too."

"Maybe for some people, but not me."

"Fine, I'm sorry I bothered you." He stepped inside far enough to lay the envelope on her kitchen island. He bent down, petted Romeo, then left.

Jewell studied the envelope addressed with her first name. She tapped her lips with her index finger.

She decided to open it.

It was an invitation reading:

Performance Celebration Picnic
  Where: Laurence Ranch, Inc.,
  2020 Sunnyside Lane,
  Crescent Beach
  When: Saturday, June 11 at Noon
  Family and Friends Welcome

She held the invitation to her chest.

∞∞∞

Jewell found it impossible to sleep. She decided to turn to her old comfort and raid the cabinets for sweets. She headed for the kitchen but froze in the doorway when she peered into the living room and kitchen. Memories flooded and bombarded her like a club over the head. She leaned in the doorway. She could see herself and Becca practicing bellydance, Becca coaching and encouraging her. She could see the two of them sitting cross-legged on the floor sipping wine and sharing their dating adventures.

She looked toward the front door and could envision Kage at the other end in his dress pants and jacket flung over his shoulder. Then she remembered his kiss, his warm passionate kiss and how she was tempted to wrap her leg around him and coax him inside. She had filled this home with an abundance of heartfelt memories in a short period of time.

She suddenly heard Taylor's voice echoing in her ears, "Nice party. You know, I bet if a person wanted to make friends and be invited to a party like that one they'd have to quit avoiding people," and, "I wanted to wish you luck in your new endeavors. I hope you find what you're looking for."

She felt foolish, Taylor meant no harm; she was trying to help her, trying to clobber advice through her thick skull.

It came to her, she still wanted these things. She had found what she was looking for and threw it away. She reviewed what she needed to do. It was foreign to her, but she needed to open up to Becca and Kage, be honest, and truly share herself. She didn't delude herself regarding the mountain ahead of her. It would be a steep climb after a lifetime of keeping things to herself.

She went to the cabinet, grabbed some cookies and stood at the counter eating and planning. She would go to the seance and join her troupe.

∞∞∞

Jewell entered the studio with uncertainty, much like the first time she had stumbled through the door.

"Well butter my butt and call me a biscuit. I thought you ran off and joined the circus," Della Rae said.

"It's about time," Maggie said. "I was fixing to take you off my list. I told you I don't chase people down."

"Man, I'm glad to lay eyes on you," Z said, as she approached Jewell and hugged her. "I texted you to check on you, didn't they come through?"

Before she answered, Sherry greeted her.

Becca stood talking with Candi and didn't acknowledge Jewell.

A hefty woman with even larger bleached-blonde hair entered the studio. The woman's hair was the kind damaged by repeated perms and chemical processing, something out of the eighties. She had a wide nose and overdone makeup of bright-blue eye shadow and pink-blush lying in circles on her cheeks where the brush plopped the color. She wore a long brown straight dress with an animal print kimono. Jewell thought she had a kind face and noted a scent of spiced cloves about her.

"Della Rae? Who is Della Rae?" the woman asked.

"I am. You must be Seana?"

"Hi, I'm Maggie, the teacher, and owner of this studio. These are my other students, Sherry, Z, Gabby, Becca, and Jewell. We are still waiting for two."

"What a pleasure to meet you." She closed her eyes and stretched her arms forward, palms turned to the ceiling. "I sense someone here with a deeper connection to the spirit. She doesn't realize the connection. Her presence has increased spiritual activity and has sparked the spirit." She opened her eyes in intense eye contact with Jewell causing her to shiver.

The thought of bolting crossed Jewell's mind as she recalled the cold breeze that had passed over her in the living room the night the mirror crashed. She also remembered the recent sense of someone following her.

"Before we commence, I want to explain what a seance involves. We are opening a portal. We will present ourselves to the spirit who exists here. We proclaim we are uninhibited and ready to receive the spirit and its message. I sense her already."

"She's a docile spirit. Della Rae has filled me in on the photo and the presumed identity of Clara Tessa Berg. We should have a positive experience and assist her on her way to the next realm."

"Many spirits are trapped and need human assistance to boost them along. Spirits are sensitive to cynical attendees and may stay away if there are any hostile or doubtful participants. Is there anyone who has reservations and would like to leave now?"

"She's not here yet," Della Rae said referring to Nicci.

"Yeah, where on earth are those two?" Maggie asked. "We'll have to start without them."

Seana used her index finger to point and count the participants in the room. "Let's see, we have seven now and multiples of three work best so I hope the other two will show."

She barely finished the sentence when Nicci arrived.

"Sorry, I was on a conference call."

"We might as well start," Maggie said.

Earlier Maggie's husband had set up a round table with nine seats. She had draped a vibrant square table cloth over it with gold tassels on all four corners. It covered a substantial portion of the table. The colors matched those of the room with the purples, pinks, and gold. Fifteen candles sat dispersed around the table.

Candi rushed in. "Wait, Gabby beat me here?"

"Yes, now get your tail in here," Maggie said.

"Let's all take a seat," Seana instructed as she pulled a loaf of bread from her cloth bag and infused the air with a fresh-baked aroma. She placed it in the center of the table. She took a chalice from the bag, opened bottled water and poured it into the silver vessel.

The group filled in around the table. Jewell made her way to the chair next to Becca, but Becca got up and moved to the other side.

"Someone please light the candles and turn out the overhead lights. We will then join hands. The strength of the group determines the strength of the seance."

Maggie flicked the lights out.

The candles cast a shadowy glow on the participants' faces. The light was brighter at their chins growing darker towards their eyes.

"We will first meditate to clear our minds of this world's chaos. Follow me. Ommmm...Ommmm...Our beloved Clara Tessa Berg, we bring you gifts from life into death. Commune with us, oh Clara, and move among us. Say it with me."

The group repeated along with her, not quite in perfect unison at first attempt jumbling the words, "Our beloved Clara Tessa Berg, we bring you gifts from life into death. Commune with us, oh Clara, and move among us."

After enough repeats, they caught onto the rhythm of the chant and reached perfect harmony until the request lifted through the room like a song.

"Our beloved Clara Tessa Berg, we bring you gifts from life into death. Commune with us, oh Clara, and move among us. Our beloved Clara Tessa Berg, we bring you gifts from life into death. Commune with us, oh Clara, and move among us."

"Hello, Clara," Seana said.

Jewell jerked. Della Rae and Z each squeezed her hand they

held.

"Please come and join us, Clara. You must be weary."

"She admits she is tired," Seana told the group. "How can we help you?"

"I neet to move on. Dere are many levels to go through, but I'm still in da first level. I didn't know how to move on until recently." Seana channeled Clara's answers in her Dutch-English dialect.

"Tell Maggie I was hanging out here because I was familiar with this studio and I was only having fun with her out of boredom."

"How can we help you move on?"

"I need to clear the trauma of my death, my murder."

Varying degrees of gasps filled the room.

"My brother has a grip on me trying to hold me here, but I didn't figure it out until the new girl came."

Jewell's face went cold as the blood rushed from it. Della Rae and Z squeezed her hands again.

"Please go on, we are here to help you."

"I've been following her, the new girl. I monitor her struggles with her brother and they opened my awareness allowing me to identify the presences of my own brother, Hanns. He has been hiding from me, pulling me down without my awareness. Once my eyes were opened to him, I started fighting his spirit. I also had to fight to keep him out of Jewell's home, but the night she stormed home upset with her brother, he was there throwing things off the shelves and around the room making a ruckus. Her dog feared his presence."

"You'll never—" Seana channeled in a distinctly different tone, a sinister-sounding deep voice then abruptly stopped.

"Oh no, I wish you hadn't spoken his name, Clara, and I wish I hadn't said it out loud."

Seana spouted commands:

"Everyone break hands!

"Stand!

"Maggie, hit the lights!

"Blow out the candles!

"Hurry!

"You'll never break away from me," Seana channeled. "Oh no, we're too late. I can't stop it."

"The lights won't come on," Maggie screeched. The only light source, the minute dim illumination from the streetlamps.

"I will, I will move on." Seana channeled the spirits and assured the group that helping the spirits articulate could escalate the finale. "Their inner struggles are taking on physical aspects drawn from the group's strength."

Jewell focused on what resembled two clouds of smoke swirling together and apart in a tornado-like formation. A whizzing sound like a freight train whirled through the room climaxing into a higher-pitched sound like the cries of two cats fighting until the clouds disappeared. A dead silence fell over the room. Maggie was able to turn the lights on.

Seana slumped. Jewell sat drained with a kind of tiredness deep in her bones. The reverential silence of the room persisted, a silence louder than any sound. When they arose, they embraced one another.

Seana beckoned them into a standing circle.

"Join hands again, please. What we witnessed was a struggle of one spirit desiring to move on to a greater spiritual level. The spirit fighting against her, her brother's spirit, does not possess the right to pass to any higher levels so he was trying to stop her. She now has command over him, being in a superior spiritual realm. She has forbidden him from coming anywhere near this group or anyone this group loves. You will be protected by Clara.

watch you from afar."

They broke the circle.

"What would it be about struggles with you and your brother, Jewell?" Maggie asked.

"I don't remember you saying anything about having a brother," Della Rae said.

"Yeah, I recall you saying you didn't have any family to speak of," Nicci said.

Jewell realized she had hit a crossroad. She weighed her options. She could forge new territory and open up to the group or keep her personal life to herself and carry on as before having superficial friendships with this group, or she could go back home, alone.

"I'm sorry I didn't tell you about him. We aren't close. We grew up in different foster homes. He lives in Washington and is three years older than me."

"That's okay, darlin', it's rough talking about those things. I had no idea you were an orphan." Della Rae wrapped her arms around Jewell.

"I think we have this resolved and there should be no more haunting here," Maggie said.

"I know it's Friday and not our usual Rhita's day, but can we all go anyway? I'll call Miranda to meet up with us," Z said. "I think we need a debriefing after this show."

Most of the group could go so they started their trek to their favorite coffee shop, only not in usual formation.

Becca walked ahead of Jewell. When they reached Rhita's, Becca turned to Jewell before entering. "See, I didn't even know you had a brother. Did I even know you at all?" She went into the coffee shop before awaiting Jewell's answer.

The group's conversation revolved around the seance.

Jewell took the opportunity to text Kage and invite him to Rhita's. She had no idea if he would respond or if he would be as icy as Becca. She was willing to accept any of his and Becca's responses since she was at fault.

"Well, I still stand by my conclusion there is no such thing as ghosts," Nicci said.

"What, how can you say that?" Della Rae asked. "After everything we witnessed tonight."

"It's simple. I am sure you filled Seana in on enough details for her to fabricate the rest. She had a play rehearsed before arriving," Nicci contended.

"Impossible. How would she have known about the night at Jewell's house?"

"Jewell probably shared it with someone, like Becca, say," Nicci said.

"No, actually, I didn't tell anyone," Jewell said, looking at Becca. Becca rolled her eyes.

"Well, she got the information somehow. Who knows, maybe she started following us after Della Rae contacted her."

"Why would she do that?" Sherry asked.

"How much did you pay her Della Rae?" Nicci asked.

"Well, I'll be. The nerve. That's between me and Maggie. We took care of it. Are you one of those characters on the cartoon? You know, the one with the dog and teenagers busting ghosts? I guess you're the smart girl with the glasses? Geez."

"All I'm saying is she may have been motivated to put on a great show so we would all refer her to others who will pay her the same."

"But what about the sounds and the smoke or clouds or whatever it was?" Z asked.

"Special effects, my dears, special effects."

"Believe what you want. I believe it was real," Jewell said.

"Coming from the scientist," Nicci said.

They gathered their things to leave. Becca went behind the counter to talk with the other staff.

Jewell opened the door to leave Rhita's only to find Kage standing on the sidewalk.

"Hey," she said.

"Hey, you," he said back.

"I wasn't sure you would come."

"I wasn't sure you would ask."

"I'm sorry—" she started, but he wouldn't let her finish. He rushed to her, placed a finger over her mouth and embraced her.

Becca descended the steps and Jewell noted her lingering, watching her and Kage.

With Becca in hearing range, Jewell said to Kage, "I understand you don't want me to apologize, but I need to. I was wrong." She glanced at Becca. "I need to tell you I've kept things from you. I want to tell you everything. Let's go back in. Maybe get some dessert." She smiled at Becca.

Jewell and Kage passed Becca on the way to the stairs.

Kage said to her, "You coming?"

The three sat at an intimate table in Rhita's near a back window with more coffee and Rhita's famous cheesecake. Jewell shared her childhood with them including the day she met Josh. She told them how Josh had been her only friend and they spent twelve years together as friends, lovers and then friends again. She told them about his struggles with phobias and his sudden death.

Kage took Jewell's hand.

Becca's shoulders softened and Jewell caught her taking a deep breath.

"And Becca, there's something I have to tell you about my brother." Jewell squirmed in her chair. She took a deep breath. "He's Nathanael. Nathanael is my brother."

"What? You've got to be kidding me. Why didn't you tell me?" Becca bolted from her chair, preparing to leave.

"Becca, stay," Kage said. "She's trying. Give her a chance."

Becca sat back down, but gazed out the window frequently.

Jewell couldn't fight her tears.

"Why did he disappear on me all of a sudden?" Becca asked. "Where is he?"

"He's back in Washington. He's not who you think he is. Yes, he's charming and handsome, but he has a dark side. I was protecting you."

"You should have told me."

"I agree. And there is more."

"More?" Becca asked.

"Yes, my mother isn't dead. My dad died like I said when I was two in a car accident. The story I've been told is my mother started drinking and couldn't handle having two kids any more so she ran off."

"Is she still living?" Kage asked.

"I have no idea. Who cares?"

"Is that everything?" Kage asked.

"No, my trip back to Washington?"

"Yes," Becca said. "Now what?"

"Well, I found Josh. He hadn't been returning my calls. I had to go check on him and I found him on the floor. He was dead."

"Dear God, Jewell," Becca said. "How could you come back and tell me it was a false alarm? I just can't understand you."

"Becca, hear her out," Kage said. "Go ahead Jewell."

"I got the report back from the medical examiner. He had a

heart condition. They think he died suddenly and didn't suffer."

"Oh sweetheart," Kage said and moved closer to Jewell to put his arm around her.

Becca sat with a blank stare and tears in her eyes.

"I promise I will try to be more open going forward, but I need your help."

"I'm in," Kage said. "What about you Becca?"

"Well, I did miss you."

"Did you go to Josh's funeral?" Becca asked.

"I plan to have a simple ceremony this Sunday. He's been cremated. I'll have to fly back to Washington. Mindy, his former assistant, and I will honor his memory and say goodbye."

"I'll go," Kage said.

"Me too," Becca said.

"That would be great."

They all stood and embraced.

Twenty-One

A Lugubrious Goodbye

Sunday morning Jewell waited for Kage and Becca but instead a Lincoln Continental pulled in front of her house. Lynn, Kage, Becca, and a young girl got out.

Jewell opened the door as they proceeded up the walkway.

"I hope you don't mind," Lynn said. "I want to go too and Brook is going to stay with Romeo."

"Oh, my groomer was going to check on Romeo, but I can call her if Brook wants to stay here and of course, I don't mind you going."

"No parties, Brook, and I mean it," Lynn said.

"I know mom, duh."

"Maybe your groomer could still come by and check on things?" Lynn whispered to Jewell.

Lynn was a woman of small stature with a few, maybe fifteen, extra pounds. She wore her short blonde hair curled under. She dressed like Jewell imagined a mom would dress in colorful loose clothing, each day with some new theme. The day's theme was sailboats and blue sneakers. An odd choice for a funeral, Jewell

168

thought, but whatever, they were going to the West Coast.

The flight and drive for this trip flew by swifter with the great company. It seemed like a flash and they were in Port Eastlyn. The rental car was better too on this trip, a comfortable SUV.

They spotted a cute young girl with shoulder-length brunette hair pacing the sidewalk as they pulled up to the funeral home. She was short with a tiny stature.

Jewell opened the door, "Mindy?"

"Ms. Jewell, Ms. Jewell, I'd recognize you anywhere from the photos Joshua kept all over the apartment." She provided a big hug.

Jewell wondered if she had been plodding through life missing how often people were hugging one another.

"Mindy, this is my best friend Becca, her mother Lynn, and my…and Kage."

"Hi, Mindy." Becca smiled at Jewell who realized she introduced her as her best friend.

She completed the obligatory paperwork and Mr. Weinbrener delivered the urn Jewell had chosen from the website. The urn reminded her of the genie's bottle Maggie's studio was patterned after. She planned to keep the urn and some of the ashes, but to sprinkle the majority off the Washington coast from a secluded area.

Jewell drove the rental car to the farthest edge of Port Eastlyn to the Sandy Point Lighthouse. Poor Becca and Kage were trapped in the back with a chatty Mindy.

The air was cool, especially for Jewell's native Floridian friends. She warned them to don their jackets. In keeping with the typical Washington coast in May, a cool breeze whipped around the shore. As the air hit her face and tousled her curls, Jewell closed her eyes to draw in the nostalgia. The scent of salty air somehow made the mix of decaying smells from decomposing seaweed and shells more tolerable.

Sentiment gripped her as she realized this could be her last visit to her hometown. With Josh gone and the strain between her and Nathanael, it was difficult to imagine anything drawing her back. She could accomplish her executor duties remotely.

They reached the final tip of land and Jewell asked if anyone wanted to say anything.

"I never met you, Josh, but I am sure you were a good person if Jewell loved you. Rest in peace," Lynn said.

Becca shook her head.

The sun beamed on the five of them but did little to warm the air.

Kage cleared his throat. "I'm sorry you had to leave this earth so early."

Jewell shifted her gaze to Mindy and expected her to tear into one of her rambles, but she kept her head down.

Lynn, the ever-ready mother, had equipped her jacket with tissues and passed them around.

Jewell closed her eyes as she inhaled a deep cleansing breath and slowly let it out. She cradled the urn in her left arm like a mother would hold a swaddled baby and with her right hand reached into her jacket pocket to retrieve the biodegradable paper inscribed with a letter to Josh.

She read:

"Josh, my first true friend. We met at a desperate time. A time when life seemed cruel and hopeless, but you were my hope, you and your soft teddy-bear embraces. You made me stronger and I often feared drawing from your strength made you weaker. I whole-heartedly wanted to fix your phobias, but you wanted something else above all,

creativity. *Be free; write your beautiful poems and prose. Dazzle the Multiverse with your soliloquy.*"

She let go of the letter and watched the wind carry it through artful formations until it landed on the water. She placed her index finger in the air to determine the direction of the wind, then removed the urn lid and freed handfuls of ashes and gave Lynn, Becca, Kage, and Mindy the same opportunity.

They left the shore, in reverent quiet.

∞∞∞

Jewell checked her tracking app. No activity showed regarding Nathanael's location. Of course, it occurred to her, his phone may be stationary, but not he.

Jewell contemplated keeping this a secret and dropping the group off at the local diner. She had it all figured out. She would tell them she had unfinished business at the funeral home and follow her tracking app to find Nathanael.

She was about to implement her plan when it dawned on her, this was part of her old behavior and her old behavior had kept her lonely.

"I have to tell you all something." Her hands were wet on the steering wheel.

"I have been following Nathanael with a tracking app. I'm aware of how it must sound, but, well, the story is a long one meant for another time, but he was harassing me and I needed to keep abreast of his whereabouts."

"What a jerk he is," Becca said.

"I need to follow where this leads in order to check on him. I can drop you all off at the diner and come back in an hour or so."

"I'm going with you," Kage said.

Jewell didn't argue.

171

She dropped the rest off at the famous town diner. Not one brick or coat of paint had changed on the place since she was a girl.

She and Kage set out to follow Nathanael's location.

She recognized the general area of Nathanael's spot on the GPS. It was in the heart of downtown, but she couldn't put her finger on the exact building as she drove toward the coordinates.

Maybe he was renting a downtown apartment. The notion seemed slim since few cheap ones remained available due to hipsters taking up renovation and infiltration.

As she rounded the block and closed in on his location, she swallowed hard, her hands gripped the steering wheel firing tension up her arms and landing on her neck.

It was the county jail. She parked and exited the car with wobbly legs. Kage followed. She pressed a button on the outside wall.

"Can I help you?" a voice echoed from the box.

"Yes, I'm Nathanael Caldwell's sister." The door buzzed and she opened it.

"Maybe I better go in alone."

"Okay, but I'll be right here," Kage assured her.

Her legs gained no strength but managed to carry her to a metal detector monitored by an armed guard.

"Empty your pockets into the container then step through. Do you have a photo ID?"

She made it to the counter where she heard the same voice who answered the call box. "Can I help you?"

"Yes, I believe my brother may be here. Nathanael Caldwell."

"He is, but visiting hours aren't until tomorrow from four to six p.m. and you have to schedule ahead of time. Would you like to schedule a visit?"

"No," she spat out, "I won't be in town. Can you tell me what charges brought him here?"

"Are you posting bail?"

"Oh heavens no. I-I just wanted to learn about the seriousness of his charges please."

"Illegal bookmaking."

"Excuse me?"

"You know, bookmaking."

Jewell's blank stare must have encouraged him to continue.

"He's been charged with six counts of first-degree promoting gambling and one count of possessing gambling records in the first degree."

"Really?"

"Yes."

"What does that mean sentencing wise?"

"Well, I shouldn't give too much information, but you seem concerned. He has a chance to make a deal. He's gotten himself tangled with a serious crime ring. If you're going out of town, you may want to stay there for a while."

"I live out of town."

"Even better."

"Look, we have video conferencing available. Let me schedule you for Saturday."

She bit her lower lip thinking it best to cut all ties now. "No thank you. And please don't tell him I was here."

"What's going on?" Kage asked when she returned to the sidewalk where he waited for her.

"He seems to be in big trouble. He got tied up in an organized crime situation. I knew he gambled but had no idea he was a bookie."

"Oh no, what are you going to do?"

"Do? I'm not going to do anything."

They met the others at the diner and Jewell and Kage ordered quick sandwiches. They needed to be at the airport shortly.

Mindy said she lived in walking distance and could walk anywhere downtown in minutes so they said their goodbyes on the sidewalk in front of the diner.

Twenty-Two

A Return to Florida with a Massage and a Kiss

*W*hen they arrived at Jewell's, Kage asked permission to stay with her awhile, saying someone in his family could pick him up later. She agreed but insisted she would drive him home.

Brook reported no parties had taken place, and the Steal family left.

"You must be exhausted," Kage said.

"You too."

"No, I didn't have the emotions you did. Let me rub your neck."

Jewell agreed. They went to the sofa and attempted various unprovocative positions for a neck massage, eventually forced into the only option of Jewell sitting between his legs.

As he started to rub with his strong farmer hands, she melded into him. She sighed and her skin tingled. She drifted into a trance. When she turned her face to Kage, they kissed.

The kissing intensified until their breathing deepened. Their hands caressed each other's body until Jewell pulled back.

"I shouldn't. The funeral is too fresh."

"I know. You're right. I'm sorry. Can we make plans for later though? I don't want to stop our momentum this time."

"I don't either. What about Saturday?"

"I'd love it."

"Okay, we'll text some ideas back and forth."

"Great plan. I'll let you rest. And really, I'll get a ride." Jewell conceded.

"Let me tuck you in. I promise I'll behave."

Her eyebrows furrowed as she flashed him a discerning glance.

"No, I promise, I will behave. Then I'll walk downtown and have my brother pick me up."

Jewell was asleep before Kage hit the front door.

∞∞∞

Saturday came, but not without frequent texting throughout the week between Jewell and Becca, and Jewell and Kage.

Becca picked Jewell up Saturday morning to head for Della Rae's where the Sisters of the Silk Veil had arranged to meet to plot their own ending choreography for the upcoming performance.

Della Rae's home was what Jewell thought of as a mansion. She thought Becca's family home was incredible, but Della Rae's trumped it by a lunar mile. Stones of tan and gold hues covered the expansive outside. Two doors, Jewell guessed were about the size of the front of her rental house, opened from the middle where the inside edges met.

The doors opened to a marble-floored foyer grand enough to land a Boeing 747. Della Rae greeted them with her abundant Southern hospitality and sweet tea.

From her cell phone, Z played the music she thought would be fun to dance to for the finale. The music was a blend of tones meshing Indonesian sounds, synthesizer, percussion, and violins. Z had been sharing the videos she was obsessed with featuring a bellydance style of Tribal Fusion. The song she chose was upbeat and circus-like, something befitting Z.

"Okay, what do you envision here?" Nicci asked.

Z said, "We'll be in a stiff formation when we end Maggie's choreography with four of us facing one way and the other three facing the opposite way. I say we shake our arms appearing to loosen up, then take it into a descending shimmy starting at our shoulders moving down to our hips. Listen, it goes with the music, she played the first few seconds. Then, we break out, I'll show you how when we're in place, but we break in different directions and improvise robot arms."

"Say what?" Sherry said.

"I made the number sweet and simple, honest," Z said, "and then we pair up facing a partner. While facing one another, we'll do mirror image snake arms, chest circles, head slides, and various hip moves. Right before the music stops, we jump as high as possible while turning to face the front. I'll try a 360 turn since I have no partner. I ran through it a couple of times, ha, then we strike a pose, any pose we want, all different. And the crowd roars."

"Okay, sounds like fun, let's work it out," Della Rae said. "Now remember, we all pinky swore, no telling husbands, boyfriends, girlfriends, children, etcetera. It needs to be a surprise for everyone."

"Oh, my kids wouldn't even listen if I told them." Gabby laughed.

"And I'm so glad you could make it Gabby and that Candi found coverage at work."

"I won't be able to next weekend. I lose commission if I'm not there. So I need to grasp this today and practice on my own," Candi said.

"And I hope I don't go home to find Kevin tied to a chair and the kids running circles around him," Gabby added.

They worked on the new choreography, then congregated in the massive outdoor area where the stone floor matching the stone on the house unfurled to the pool and beyond. The water in the expansive pool beamed pristine in the sunshine.

"Like, where's your family?" Candi asked.

"The kids are out running around as usual and Winslow, why, the heavens above only know his whereabouts." Della Rae said through clenched teeth, "Running around too, as usual, I suppose."

They thanked Della Rae for her hospitality and praised her gorgeous home.

Becca dropped Jewell off and wished her luck for her date with Kage.

∞∞∞

Through their texting during the week, Jewell and Kage had settled their plans on a trip to Southbridge Beach to have dinner followed by a barefoot stroll on the beach. He insisted upon these plans when he learned she hadn't spent much time on the beach yet, something he struggled to comprehend.

It was a warm night. Jewell noted the days were heating up and she had to keep the top of her Beetle up and run the AC, something she hated. She was also more diligent about making sure Romeo had cool water.

They enjoyed dinner on the deck of the restaurant, the sea breeze gentle and soothing. Kage stared as Jewell's hair fluttered.

Later, the warm ocean water crashed at their feet as they strolled hand in hand. Her dress blew about her thighs. Jewell reasoned she was lost in a dream.

"Are you feeling better about things? I mean Josh."

"I am. The fact I have you and Becca is helping."

"I'm glad. You never said, are you coming to Mom's picnic the day after the performance? You *are* the motivating factor for this party."

"Really?"

"Yes, really. I was wondering if you would be willing to visit the farm the night of the performance. We could go out to eat first followed by a drive to the farm. It'd be good for you to meet them first, before the picnic."

They agreed on the plan and made their way back to Kage's truck. They clapped their shoes together to shake off the sand and brushed it off their feet.

"Want to ride around or go back to your place?"

She shot him a sly look and answered they should go to her place. Resistance would take no part in this evening.

The return trip over the bridge, into downtown and then to her house seemed an eternity. Country music played on his radio. Songs about love. He reached over and placed his hand on her leg. She feared the heat between their bodies would combust, setting the truck seat ablaze. Their intense attraction reminded her of how massive objects in space orbit each other creating big waves and big sounds.

They scarcely made it through her front door before he placed his hands on the sides of her face and leaned down, his lips near hers. She closed her eyes.

"Is it still too soon?"

"No," she answered in a breathy voice, her eyes closed and face turned up toward him.

They began kissing softly. His fingers ran through her hair

and behind her head. Her breathing hastened and she kissed him fiercely. She stroked the firm muscles of his arms and then stood on her tiptoes to wrap her arms around his broad back. He squeezed her buttocks and drew her closer. Blood coursed through her veins, heated blood with the power to prick nerve endings back to life.

With her chest heaving from breathlessness, she stepped back from him never breaking eye contact. She slipped out of her shoes and unbuttoned her dress.

Kage ripped his shirt off and tugged at his boots. He lost his balance forcing him to hop several feet to avoid falling before landing hard against the counter.

Jewell laughed so hard she had to double over.

"Oh you think that was funny, do you?" He scooped her into his arms and carried her to the bedroom. He closed the door with his foot, leaving Romeo on the other side.

"Sorry buddy," he called to him as the door swung shut.

They awoke to the sun shining through the window and Romeo whining.

"Oh no, we better let him in." Kage sprang from the bed.

Jewell sat up, pushed the hair from her face and focused on Kage rambling to the door, naked.

He glanced back. "Hey, no peeking."

∞∞∞

The next weekend played out similarly to the last. The troupe spent more hours together practicing and catching on to Z's choreography. Jewell and Kage enjoyed a weekday lunch together, thanks to the rain gods. Lacey gave Jewell thumbs up for the return of her cowboy.

Jewell and Kage's Saturday date started early. He wanted to show her the tourist attractions she had never visited. Their evening ended the same as the previous Saturday night, only this time they opened the door after their lovemaking to let Romeo in to sleep with them.

Twenty-Three

A Performance with a Twist

~Ȿ~

*T*he night of the long-awaited performance finally arrived. Jewell double checked her bag before heading to the studio: Costume, check, makeup, check, jewelry, check. She determined her packing complete.

Only one more task to complete, stop at the post office on her way to the studio. The promised check secure in the registered-mail envelope addressed to Oliver and Timpleton Research, Port Eastlyn, WA. The postal clerk advised her on the safest way to send a large check. Jewell donated a generous portion of Josh's estate to Oliver and Timpleton to continue the promising research to treat phobias and to draw a dose of redemption. Only she and Nathanael knew the truth.

She set aside another portion of Josh's wealth to fund Mindy's college degree. She retained just enough for herself to secure her future. Besides, she was skilled at investing.

Female voices buzzed through the studio dressing room with chatter and laughter as the dancers hustled and bustled to ready themselves. Della Rae fastened Jewell's bra/bedla as she adjusted

182

the front hoping nothing, albeit a small nothing, would fall out during a twist or turn.

Sherry searched her bag with frenzy for costume pieces and Candi stood sideways in self-admiration hogging the only semi-full-length mirror in the room. She stood with her arm bent at the elbow and forearm thrown behind her head in a seductive pose.

Nicci rolled her eyes at the sight.

The only non-troupe member in the room was Miranda, there to assist Z, who never fussed over wardrobe. She grumbled at Miranda's insistence on applying makeup for a final touch, giving them all a dose of amusement while serving to relieve tension.

Jewell practiced taking deep breaths. The breaths did little to alleviate her anxiety, as she replayed mental images of tripping or of going left when everyone else went right.

"Jewell, are you okay?" Becca asked. "You look like you're going to hyperventilate."

"Come here," Becca said. "Candi, move over, we all know you're gorgeous."

"See." Becca stood Jewell in front of the mirror and pulled her hair back. "Behold this stunning costume and the beautiful woman in it." She lowered her voice for only Jewell to hear. "That's the dancer you told me you read about as a little girl."

Jewell's body relaxed.

Candi peeked through the dressing room door and announced the attendees. "There are at least a dozen people out there."

"Let me see," said Becca. "I spy my mom, dad, and Brook. Oh, and Kage." She smiled back towards Jewell. "I see Candi's parents and new beau, Della Rae's family, and Nicci's husband. Who's coming for you Sherry?"

"No one, but I'm fine."

"You have us."

Maggie had set up folding chairs prompted by the undesirable prospect of watching out-of-shape guests navigate floor cushions.

Jewell listened as hypnotic Egyptian tunes floated into the dressing room. Earthy scents of burning incense drifted from the studio.

They had closed the door to take one last check of each other when Maggie barged in.

Miranda snagged the opportunity to dash to an open seat.

"Ready?" Maggie asked, followed by instructions, "Once you hear me announce your troupe and Tabla Solo come out in the order we rehearsed. Wait, get in line now in order. This isn't right." She arranged them by height, tallest to shortest. Nicci, Candi, Becca, Jewell, Sherry, Della Rae, Z, and Gabby.

Maggie spoke into a microphone lending an official air to the performance. "Friends, family, and supporters welcome to The Sacred Veil Studio. I'm Maggie of the Silk Veil. Tonight my beautiful beginner troupe will showcase all their hard work and perform to an Egyptian piece, Tabla First Solo. I am pleased to present the Sisters of the Silk Veil."

Gabby opened the door to the sound of applause and the troupe promenaded to the dance floor in the prescribed order.

Jewell scanned the audience and her eyes landed on Kage who nodded his head and applauded in support. He placed two fingers in his mouth and blasted a whistle. Jewell's plastered-on nervous smile thawed into a more natural one. She reminded herself this was for enjoyment and no one could shoot her if she screwed up. She remembered Maggie's coaching. "If you mess up, keep on going and don't react. No one will even notice."

The three-minute dance somehow seemed an eternity and a

blur all at the same time. When the Tabla First Solo number ended, Miranda played Z's Tribal Fusion song using her cell phone and amplifier.

Sisters of the Silk Veil shook their arms and launched into the shimmies arranged in Z's choreography. The dance was fun and flew by as the troupe smiled and laughed.

When the music stopped and they struck their unique poses. The crowd applauded and then stood intensifying their applauses, whistles and calls. The troupe stepped to the back of the performance area in their beginning formation, their expressions beaming.

Maggie took her place in front of them and raised the microphone to her lips. "Well, I never thought I'd witness the day Tribal would be danced in this studio, but I'll tell you what, these women rocked it and I'm proud to say they're my students. Look at y'all coming up with your own choreography after only beginner classes. Amazing."

The troupe gestured the attention to Z.

A reception followed the performance and Kage raced to Jewell's side where he planted himself for the remainder of the celebration. Jewell drew comfort from the closeness and carried no objections. There was something about his body heat.

They met Becca's dreamy father, Mitch, with his gray hair, blue eyes, and fine build. He was dressed in a suit not having had time to change after work.

The event provided the opportunity to meet each other's significant others. Nicci's husband, Levon, was tall, handsome, and distinguished in his expensive-looking trousers and lavender polo shirt, a perfect complement to Nicci's purple costume. Jewell suspected the matching was no accident.

They finally got to meet the infamous Winslow Young, a

dashing white-haired man. Jewel studied him as she remembered Della Rae's implicit comment about him while sitting on their back patio by the pool.

Gabby's husband, Kevin, was able to make the performance. He had somehow convinced Gabby's parents to watch the kids. Jewell was certain begging and bribes factored in somewhere.

He was a kind-looking man in his early-thirties, a little over-weight with little sense of style, yet a dedicated father and husband according to Gabby's stories.

Becca leaned into Jewell. "Can you believe Candi is still dating the broke guy?"

"No, I can't. I guess she's keeping him until the right rich one comes along." They nodded in agreement. Candi had been dating the same one she had literally bumped into at the tavern the night of their "dance party." Tom was six-foot-two with massive muscles and tight buns, but hardly Candi's future type, given his position as a local mechanic.

The reception wound down and Jewell left with Kage for dinner and then the trip to the farm.

As they drove the main drag to Crescent Beach, Kage pointed out where his family's property began just to her right. The miles stretched and the drive continued as they passed acre after acre.

"Still our land to your right."

She watched as they passed row after row of crops, crops of wide leafy green plants with a similar appearance to cabbage, but not exactly.

"Is the crop bok choy?"

"Wow. Very good. For generations, our family grew various vegetables, spotlighting potatoes, and we maintained livestock. We made a living from it, but the soil changed, became sandier. We researched and learned to adapt and our farm is still operational because of it. Many went under. Plus the value of our land is astronomical. We receive offers weekly if not daily from developers wanting us to sell, but grandpa always asks, "If we sell our land, where do they think we're going to live?"

Jewell giggled at Kage's imitation of his grandfather's voice.

As they turned onto the paved road leading to the homes, he explained there were three houses. His family lived in the primary house, leaving the smaller one-story home for his grandparents and the middle home for his Uncle John and family.

He continued to explain the larger family who bore the bulk of the work, which happened to be his family, stayed in the center house.

Jewell listened with complete adoration as Kage described his life.

She developed an appreciation for what she had considered an archaic lifestyle and marveled over his unique outlook she assumed few his age would embrace. She figured most in his situation would pester the life out of their family to sell the farm and buy a beach house.

As the truck approached Kage's family house, he explained how all events were held at the main house. That was part of the deal and the entire family even from the other homes would be there to meet Jewell.

"Oh great, no pressure there."

"Nah, you'll be fine. Except..."

"Except what?"

"Well, I've bragged you up so much, you may have difficulty living up to your own image."

"Great."

"No, I'm teasing."

Relief pervaded as Jewell learned her vision of the main house was far from the truth. She had somehow conjured an image of a dilapidated, dirty whitewashed house sitting apologetically on massive acreage with some of its shutters hanging unhinged.

Instead, it was a three-story home of overwhelming size. It was covered in classic gray shingles and trimmed in white. The porch was expansive yet inviting. It wrapped around the front and both sides of the house with white rockers spread throughout. One corner of the porch jetted into a gazebo.

As they approached the stairs, the family poured out of the home overtaking the expansive porch.

"Everyone, this is Jewell. Jewell, this is my mom, Liz."

His mother, who headed the group, was a simply gorgeous woman with glowing skin, hazel eyes, soft light brown hair pulled back and full lips providing a wide friendly smile showing off her white teeth. The woman's beauty came as no surprise, given Kage's good looks.

"This is my dad, David."

He was a man with bulging muscles who looked the part of someone who had been working on a farm his entire life. His hair was balding, but his kind brown eyes and plump cheeks helped him hang on to his good looks.

The introductions went on to include his siblings Alexia, at age sixteen, ten years Kage's junior, and Hayden, only two years younger. Alexia was a lucky girl who had clearly inherited both recessive genes, supplying her with light brown hair and green eyes. Hayden was a younger version of his father.

Jewell met Kage's grandparents, a couple in their sixties and in no way past it. She detected a theme of good looks running through this family.

Next, she met his Uncle John and Aunt Deborah with their son Michael who Jewell would guess to be around Kage's age sporting the same soft curls.

"Y'all come in for dessert," Liz summoned.

Jewell sized up the dining room and considered it big enough to plop her whole house in. It contained a sturdy table capable of seating this entire clan with room for additions. They dug into lemon meringue pies, pies with peaks nearly as high as the eighteen-foot ceilings.

"Jewell, I'm so thrilled you're coming to the picnic tomorrow. You'll have a blast, I promise. I love to entertain," Kage's mother, Liz, said.

"Oh, I appreciate the invitation and the invitation to the whole troupe. I can't wait."

"Not only the troupe, but their families too. Our back lawn will be filled with folks tomorrow and I love it," Liz said.

"Me too," Kage's grandmother said.

"Should I bring anything?"

"No dear, we'll provide everything," Liz said.

"Do you see these pies?" Kage asked, using his fork to point. "You haven't seen anything yet."

Twenty-Four

A Picnic Does a Saturday Make

*T*he back screen door slammed behind Liz as she carried trays down the steps into the expansive yard filled with picnic tables, lawn chairs, and mingling guests. Jewell scurried to lend her a hand and hooked a tray overflowing with an assortment of fresh fruits.

Kage and his father tended the grill. It emitted the delectable aroma of burgers and hot dogs through the air compelling Romeo to visit them frequently to check on the progress.

Romeo bounced to Jewell's side, bringing his two new friends in tow. Lynn and Becca were inspired by Romeo to get their own standard poodles. The two were littermate pups only twelve weeks old. Percival was white with a splash of black on his chest and Genevieve was pure white

Lynn ran around the yard trying to catch the pups to feed them, but Genevieve and Perci had no intentions of being caught.

Jewell scanned the well-manicured lawn filled with her friends as satisfaction and contentment seeped through her whole being. She inspected the guests and Kage's family dressed in their bright clothing and chills enveloped her when she watched Liz who reminded her of the woman on the cover of the magazine she had picked up in the grocery store checkout line a lifetime ago. Liz stood wearing her apron with her arms folded as she winked at Jewell over the success of the picnic.

This omen convinced her that her move to Southbridge and journey with her new friends were meant to be all along. It was written in the stars.

She experienced an overwhelming sense of being watched from above. She paused and stared at the sky with its light blue backing and billowy white clouds. The revelation of Clara and Josh looking down upon her warmed Jewell as if she were being wrapped in a warm blanket doused with the scents of vanilla and cinnamon.

"Be happy Josh, be happy," she whispered for the wind to carry.

About the Author

Hi, I'm Cathryn Petit and I sincerely hope you have enjoyed reading the story of Jewell Caldwell and her new friends as much as I enjoyed writing it. Reviews are crucial for any author, and even just a line or two can make a huge difference. I would greatly appreciate a review on Amazon or any of your other favorite sites. In addition, your review can help other readers decide to pick up this book and enjoy it as well. Thank you in advance.

I know you don't want to miss the second book in this series: *A Spell of Wanderlust*, which is well underway and set for publication later in 2019. Act now to receive notifications regarding the upcoming launch date for this exciting second book by connecting with me on my website or Facebook page provided here.

You can connect with me on:

◓ https://www.cathrynlynnpetit.com

⬛ https://www.facebook.com/Cathryn-Lynn-Petit-Author-291808888393612

Subscribe to my newsletter:

✉ https://www.cathrynlynnpetit.com/contact

Made in the USA
Columbia, SC
29 June 2019